4 EVER DOWN WITH HIM

TAY MO'NAE

CHAPTER 1

*K*ingston "Nike" Trollvier
 "I don't understand why I can't go with you Nike,"
Evelynn whined.

I grabbed my pants, put them on and sighed before looking at her. Eve was a beautiful woman. But that's all she was; She was about 5'4 light skinned chick with dimples so deep you can swim in them. She was stacked and shaped perfectly like a coke bottle, with an ass just like Nicki. She worked at a local hair salon but had no ambition about her. She used it as a side hustle why her main hustle was getting money from different niggas.

My nigga Duke was throwing a party for his 25th birthday at *LIV*, and it was gonna be epic. Duke had rented out the whole damn club, and it was always a good time when my niggas and I had an event and the whole city showed up.

"Evelynn, why, the fuck would we go to a party together like we're a fucking couple?" I grabbed my shirt and put it on and began walking towards her dresser to grab my phone and weed without waiting for her to answer.

"But we can be, I don't understand how I'm good enough to spend the night with and shit, but I can't go out in public with you."

I ran my hand over my hair growing impatient with this conversation.

"Look, I told you last time if you can't handle just fucking we need to cut ties. I'm not for this extra shit. Go to the damn party and have a good time but we're not going together."

This time I didn't wait for her to reply. Instead, I headed to the front of her one-bedroom apartment and put my shoes on and headed out the door.

I headed down the stairs as the Miami heat hit me and jogged over to my 2017 Maserati Ghibli.

Now I know what y'all thinking how, at the age twenty-five, how could a nigga own a Maserati and had a friend that could rent out a damn nightclub. But it's simple we were some young bosses and we made shit happen. I owned two of the most successful car detailing shops in Miami for exotic cars, *Deluxe Wheels*, not to mention, I used to sell the purest dope you could find in the south, but I realized I didn't want the drug game anymore and decided to focus more on my detailing shops. Duke still had parts in it, but that was all him.

I started my car and headed towards my house. I had some hours to kill before the party tonight, so I needed to shower, change and go check on my shops.

I pulled into my two-story brick modern day home and parked in the driveway. I was truly living good. I had come from middle class and upgraded. My house was a 4 bedroom, 3 ½ baths. It also had a theater room, game room, and an underground and outdoor pool. It wasn't anything extraordinary, but it was something.

As I was getting out, the car my phone began to vibrate. Looking down, I seen it was Evelynn. I sighed and ignored her call and put my shit in my pocket. I walked up to the door and opened it when it started vibrating again.

Not even bothering to look I walked in my house and headed straight towards my bedroom and immediately took my phone out my pocket and tossed it on my bed. I stripped out my clothes and threw them into my clothes hamper and went and got in the shower.

Since I had a lot of running around to do, I put on my grey Nike sweat suit with a pair of all white Forces, in case y'all were wondering why I was called Nike, it was because that's all I rocked when I was younger, and people started calling me it, and it stuck.

I was looking in my mirror and made a mental note to get lined up before tonight even though bitches were still gonna flock to me even with my hair untamed.

I was far from an ugly nigga. I'm 6'2 and 190 athletic built, I used to live in the gym when I had time and played ball and even though I didn't go as much I still had the muscle from it. With my dark brown skin, big pink lips, right dimple, and afro tapered hair, I was the shit. I kept my beard long and it was usually wild looking, but the bitches loved running they hands through it. The top part of my body was covered with tattoos, I had them on my neck, chest, arms, a nigga was addicted.

Once I was dressed and ready to go, I grabbed my phone and looked at it. I had a bunch of miss calls and texts from Evelynn and a call from Duke. Erasing all Evelynn's stuff, I hit Duke back.

"What's up nigga?" I said.

"Where yo pretty boy ass at Nike?" He said laughing.

"Fuck you nigga; I'm about to stop by my shop, then the barbershop, and then head yo way."

"Bet." He said and hung up.

I grabbed my keys headed out my room down the stairs and then out the door after locking my door. I took out my iPhone 7 Plus and went to my security system app, for my house, and set the alarm. Once I made sure my house was cool, I went to my car and started and headed towards one of my detail shops.

I was sitting at my desk going over numbers, getting my deposits ready for both shops, when the door busted open. I instantly reached for my gun in the holster on the side of the inside of my desk and pointed it at the door.

"Nike, what the fuck!" Trina yelled.

"Trina why the fuck you just busting in here without knocking," I said, putting my gun back in place.

"I called you, but you didn't answer. So, I called Duke, and he said you were here."

I reached in my desk drawer and looked at my phone, and sure enough Trina had called me. I had put my phone on silent because Evelynn's dumbass wouldn't stop calling me.

"What's up Trina? What you need, some money?"

She smacked her lips and rolled her eyes.

"Big brother, do you think I only come to you when I want money?"

I laughed and shook my head. "Hell, yeah man, why else would you pop up on me for no reason.

"Maybe because I heard something you might want to hear too."

I stopped counting my money and looked up at her. I wasn't sure were this conversation was going, but I was sure I wouldn't like it.

"What?"

"Shonni is back in town."

It's like time stopped when she said that. Shonni or Noni as she liked being called was my baby, well she wasn't my baby, but we knew the deal, rather I did. Noni was 5'5, light skinned, with the darkest brown eyes kind of looked black depending on the lighting. She has the finest body I had ever seen, 36 C boobs that made me want to pull them out and suck on them every time I thought about her, with a slim ass waist and fat ass booty. Her body reminded me of J-Lo's and thanks to her running track her stomach was surf board flat.

Back in the day, Noni was not only a track star, but she was a fucking science genius. Her only down fall was that she was so caught up with track and her precious science experiments that she wouldn't give any niggas any time of day. I had practically grown up with Noni, being she was my sister's best friend. She was three years younger than me and her young ass had me gone soon as she hit puberty, and her ass started filling out.

Long story short, I was a jackass in high school and some niggas I played ball with made a bet that I couldn't break Noni in and my dumb ass never turned down a challenge and after a year of "dating her," I finally broke her ass in. Only thing wrong with that is I had a whole ass girlfriend, Chyna, and let's just say once Noni found out and I was not her favorite person at all.

"Word? How you know that?" I asked smoothly.

"She hit me up, even though I promised not to tell you she wanted to meet up with me. She is or was my best friend before you fucked up, twice!"

Oh, yeah, I did fuck with her again after that night I took her virginity, but that's another story.

I tugged at my beard and stared at my sister for a minute.

"I know I fucked up and I promise to make it right whenever I see her."

"Yeah, you better, I miss my best friend." With that, she turned and walked out the door.

I pushed my chair back and ran my hand threw my hair and thought back to the last time I seen Noni. I had fucked up with her royally, but a nigga was much wiser, and as much as I wanted to act like she ain't mean shit to me, Noni was my world. It crushed me when she left town, but at the time I knew I was no good for her. But now, I'm ready, and she had no choice but to be with me.

I looked at my phone and seen I had three hours before we were meeting up to pregame, so instead of going to my second shop, like I planned, I texted one of my managers and told him to check things out and I would get with him tomorrow and I headed home.

I got home and grabbed my wave cap and wrapped it around my head so I wouldn't mess up my braid. After replying to a few text messages, I put my phone on silent and laid down in my bed and instantly fell asleep.

❀

*A*fter I woke up, I got into the shower. Dressed in some all-white Gucci pants with an all-white Gucci button down and my all white retro 4s, I walked over to my dresser and grabbed my gold cross chain and my Rolex and my phone and headed out the door.

CHAPTER 2

Shonni "Noni" Knight

"Kingston stop running before you fall and hurt your-self!" I yelled at my 3-year-old son, while my sister yanked my head.

"Noni, stop moving before I burn your ass." She said.

"I'm sorry that I need to make sure my son is okay," I said rolling my eyes.

"Girl he's fine, Jayceon's little bad ass got him." She said referring to her five-year-old son.

I laughed, if Jay had him them that meant my son was doomed. I loved my nephew, but lord knows he was bad as hell.

"So, are you going to Duke's party?" She asked me.

I didn't answer right away. Instead, I twiddled my hands and chewed at my bottom lip. Something I always did when I was nervous.

"I don't know yet, Lo," I said lowly.

"Girl bye, you better, don't let that man keep you from enjoying yourself, plus your home for good and you need to tell him."

I sighed knowing she was right. My eyes traveled over to Kingston, or KJ as I sometimes called him before I answered.

"How the hell do I tell him that not only did he fuck and play me twice, but the second time we created a child together. A child I hid from him and moved away with."

I began to tear up and quickly wiped my eyes.

Lo put the flat iron down and sat by me on the couch and wrapped her arms around me.

"Noni, I know it hurts, and I know why you moved, but you have to think of KJ he deserves to know his father and Nike deserves to know y'all have a kid together, plus if Deshawn comes looking for you, you're going to need all the help you can."

She was right, Deshawn was the reason why I came back home. After completing high school and getting pregnant, my ass moved to Atlanta where I attended Spelman University and got my Bachelor's degree in chemistry and police science.

I would have stayed and got my Masters but my ex-boyfriend Deshawn couldn't keep his hands to himself, and after a few fractured ribs, broken nose, and too many black eyes, I gathered my son and came back home where I planned on enrolling in Miami University to get my Masters.

"I know, I know, and I'm going to tell him. I wrote Trina and told her I wanted to meet up with her tomorrow, so I'll break the news to her first and then move on from there."

She shook her head but didn't comment instead she stood up and finished my hair.

"Bitch we're going to that party. I'm not straightening all this hair for no reason."

I laughed, she was right my hair was long as fuck. It went down to the middle of my back when straighten which wasn't often because it took forever.

"Fine, mommy already agreed to keep KJ tonight, so I guess I'll go."

"Yes, bitch we about to go get yo baby daddy back."

&

"*N*oni hurry up damn, by the time you're finished the damn party is gonna be over," Lo yelled.

I rolled my eyes and checked myself out in the full body mirror hanging in her bathroom.

I had on an all nude bodycon dress with a deep cut down the center that ended at my belly button. Thank God, all those years of track helped keep my body in tack after my pregnancy. I had on light make up enough to make my face pop, but not enough to notice. I applied my lip gloss and walked out the bath room and down the hall where Lo was on the couch on her phone.

"It's about time." She said.

"Damn Lo chill, no one goes to a party when it first starts," I said putting on my all black red bottoms.

"Bitch this is Duke's party, you know how packed this party is about to be."

"Chill, we're good."

I looked at her, and she was wearing a red body pants suit and with some olive colored heels.

Loranda, or Lo was five years older than me, but she was my best friend. Standing at 5'8 her dark chocolate skin, she inherited from her father, glowed as always. I always told Lo she should model. She wasn't the thickest female, but she was definitely slim thick, and with her shoulder length hair that was currently hidden by the bundles in her hair she could put all the girls on *American's Next Top Model* to shame. Her dad was Jamaican, he was killed when she was three, but she inherited a lot of his features as well as our mom's Italian and black facial features.

I grabbed my car keys, and my LV wristlet and headed towards the door. Going to my 2015 Honda Civic, I opened the door and waited for Lo to lock her door and get in the car.

I looked over at her and took a deep breath this was going to be a long night, especially when I ran into Nike.

After valet parked my car, Lo and I walked up to the door, and the line was wrapped around the door but thank God, a dude Lo used to date was working the door because there was no way I was waiting in line.

We walked up to him and before he even looked at us, he told us back on the line.

"Come on Kyle are you really going to make me wait in line," Lo said.

He whipped his head up and showed all 32 teeth.

"Shit what's up Lo." He said looking her up and down licking his lips.

"I'm trying to get in the party, but that won't happen if I got to wait in line."

"Bitch you gotta get in line just like the rest of us!" A random girl yelled.

Kyle chuckled and moved over. "You and yo sister go ahead in."

Lo and I looked back at the girl and I blew a kiss out. "Dumb bitch." I mumbled.

We walked in, and *Young M.A* was blasting through the speakers. "Come on let's head to the bar," Lo said practically dragging me.

"Let me get two Blue Mutha fuckas!" She yelled to the bartender.

"OKAY, LADIES AND GENTLEMEN THE MAN OF THE HOUR HAS ARRIVED!" The DJ stopped the music and yelled through the mic. The lights dimmed, and the spot light hit the front entrance and in walked Duke, Nike, Trina, and the rest of their crew, the crowd spread like Moses was walking through. Everyone was admiring how good the crew looked, but I was only admiring Nike. I swear if I could, I would fuck him right there in the doorway. He was wearing all white and was looking all heavenly.

"Noni, wipe yo damn mouth," Lo said laughing, snapping me out my trance.

I shook my head and looked at her before focusing back on Nike. They headed straight to the stairs that led to the VIP section, and when he finally disappeared out of sight, it was like I could breathe again.

Lo nudged me and handed me my drink, and I swear I drunk it in less than five minutes. I was so nervous from seeing Nike that I need something stronger.

I turned around and faced the bartender and asked for double shot of Patron. After receiving it and throwing back, I grabbed Lo's hand and told her I wanted to dance.

It's like soon as I hit the dance floor the ratchetness started. *Back That Azz Up* blared through the club, and I was feeling the Patron shots, and I bent down and placed my hands on my knees and began backing my ass up. Someone came behind me and grabbed my waist, but I didn't even look to see who it was, all I know was, I was being hyped up by my sister and everyone behind me and was starting to loosen up.

After a while, I got tired and pulled away from the guy and turned to walk away. I looked up at the VIP section, and my heart began beating out of my chest. Looking down at me with a look that could kill was Nike. I gulped and quickly grabbed Lo's hand and made my way back to the bar.

CHAPTER 3

*N*ike
    I pulled into Duke's house and seen most of our crew was there. I parked my car, got out, and walked up to the door. I walked in the house and headed straight back to the stairs that led to Duke's finished basement and bar.

"Nigga I could have come in and robbed yo ass," I yelled smiling at Duke's already drunk ass.

"My nigga, I knew yo ass was on the way and unlocked the door." He said laughing.

"Yeah, alright." I walked over to the bar where Trina was sitting on one of the stools and grabbed the bottle of Henny out the ice.

"Who the hell you over here texting?" I said kissing her cheek and trying to look at her phone.

She laughed and snatched her phone back. "Nobody nosey," She said. I looked at her knowingly, but let it go. Trina was my heart and even though she was grown, she still my baby sister and I would body anybody over her, no questions asked. I looked over at her and frowned.

"Yo, what the fuck do you got on," I said mugging her.

"Nike, leave me alone nothing is wrong with that I am wearing." She said waving me off.

I grabbed her wrist and pulled her up. Her shirt was cut down to her damn belly button, and her damn shorts were halfway up her ass.

"Trina, I swear yo ass is gonna make me go to jail tonight." She once again waved me off.

"Nigga, leave Trina's sexy ass alone and come get in this rotation," Duke said.

I side eyed him. "Nigga, what I tell you about saying that smart shit about my sister?"

He laughed and wrapped his arm around my shoulder. "Chill, you know that's baby sis. But she is finer than a mutha fucker."

"Where the fuck is the blunt. I need to get high before I punch yo dumbass." Duke laughed and let me go and walked over to where a few of our niggas had a few blunts going. I took another shot of the Henny before I sat down and grabbed the blunt.

After an hour, we were all fucked up, besides Trina, she was going to be our DD so even though she was high she was fully operational.

"Aye before we walk out this bitch everyone raise they bottles. I said. Happy Birthday to my nigga since 3rd grade, my muthafucking brother!" We all yelled and took and drank of our bottles and then headed upstairs to the cars.

When we got to the club after pre-gaming of course, the bitch was already rocking and almost at capacity, and it had only been going for two hours. We headed right to our VIP section and this nigga Duke was fucked up.

I had to laugh because soon as the bottle girls walked over with the Henny I asked to be delivered when we arrived, Duke grabbed one of them and pulled her onto his lap and started motor boating her chest.

I didn't even say anything because Duke didn't give a fuck. Plus, the bitch didn't move or complain so fuck it.

I was enjoying myself and was scoping out the scene looking at the bitches who were lucky enough to get past security and come into our sections. I had a girl who name I didn't catch on my lap dancing to *Back That Azz Up*. She was okay in the face and had a fat ass. If she played her cards right I might bless her with this dick tonight.

I looked over at Trina, and she motioned me to come over to the railing she was standing over. She always observed the crowd before she went and joined the main crowd.

"Watch out little mama," I said gently pushing the girl to the side.

"Where are you going, Nike?" She asked grabbing me.

"Bitch, would you just move," I yelled pushing her again this time a little harder.

I stood up and straightened out my pants and walked over to where my sister was. "What's up?" She didn't say anything instead she pointed and turned and walked away. I looked in the direction she was pointing, and I instantly seen red.

There was Noni, my Noni, shaking her ass on some clown ass nigga. I stood there and folded my arms and watched her resisting the urge to go snatch her ass up! When the song was over, or rather she was done dancing, she finally pulled away from dude, and like a magnet, her eyes wondered up and landed on me, and it was like she seen a ghost.

I turned around to find Trina and walked over to her. "Go to talk to her," I said sitting down by her.

"No, you go talk to her." She said, not looking up from her phone.

"Come on Trina you told me to fix it, and I'm trying to."

"Fine, but not right now. Let Noni enjoy her night, and I'll find her before we leave."

I smiled and got up and went to sat back down by the big booty girl who was dancing on me before; shorty was definitely gonna have to help me after seeing Noni, my dick instantly bricked up.

I grabbed her hand and moved it over to my dick and looked at her and she had the look of shock and lust in her eyes. She licked her lips, and that was all conformation I needed. I grabbed her hand and headed to the VIP bathroom but after knocking and realizing that someone as in it, I decided to go downstairs and take her in the main bathrooms.

After leading shorty through the crowd and to the bathrooms, I walked and went to the biggest stall and shut and locked it. Ol' girl instantly dropped down to her knees and started to unzip my pants and pulling them down along with my boxers and stuffed my whole 9 ½ inches in her mouth.

I might have not known her name, but the way she was sucking my dick, I might have to learn it and keep her around.

Once I got myself together me and deep throat, or Sharee, I learned her name was headed out the bathroom. Just as we were walking past the women's bathroom, someone hurried out bumping right into me.

"Damn bitch watch where you're going!" Sharee yelled trying to grab my hand. I yanked it back and looked at her ready to strangle her before focusing back in front of me.

"I'm sorry." She whispered and tried to walk away quickly, but I grabbed her little ass and pulled her back into me.

"King, please let me go." She said trying to pull away and stumbling. Her ass drunk as shit.

"Noni, I'll never let you go," I said staring in her eyes.

I looked her over and licked my lips. She was wearing the fuck out the dress she had on. I pulled back a little to give her a good look over, and her ass had gotten much thicker since the last time I seen her.

I gently yanked her into me and wrapped my arms around her and sniffed her hair, which smelled fruity as hell.

I had forgotten Sharee was there until she cleared her throat.

"Bitch don't you see I'm busy. Get the fuck on!" I said never losing my grip on Noni.

"Nike who is this bitch?" She said.

I let go of Noni with one arm and turned and look at Sharee.

"She's someone you better not ever disrespect again, or I'll fuck you up."

Instead of replying, she rolled her eyes and walked away. I turned my focus back on Noni and tried to meet her stare, but she was looking everywhere but at me.

"It's been almost four years Noni, where the fuck you been?" I asked looking her over again.

She shrugged her shoulders and replied. "School."

"Noni!" Someone yelled her name. We both turned and looked, and it was Lo.

"Lo Lo, what's up?" I smiled and let go of Noni to hug her.

"Hey Nike, it's nice seeing you again." She said.

"CAN WE GET THE BIRTHDAY BOY TO THE STAGE!" The DJ announced.

"Shit seeing yo beautiful ass made me forget I was here for my brother's birthday." I said pulling away from Lo, and looking at Noni.

She didn't say anything. Instead, she played with her fingers and bit her lip. I smirked, she still did that shit when she was nervous.

"Can we meet and talk soon?" I asked.

"King I-." She started but was cut off by Lo.

"Come by my house tomorrow and bring Trina. I miss her little crazy ass. I have her on Facebook, so I'll message her the address and come around three, cool?"

"Good look Lo, now let me go see my boy get his surprise, I'll see y'all tomorrow." I walked over to Noni and kissed her forehead and turned and walked away.

I walked back in to the main crowd and smiled as I seen my nigga head on stage and sit in the chair that was placed in the middle. I walked closer to the stage to get a better look and me and him made eye contact, and I shrugged.

"She got a big booty so I call her Big Booty
Skrt skrt...wrists moving, cooking, getting to it
I'm in the kitchen, yams everywhere
Just made a juug, I got bands everywhere
You the realest nigga breathing if I hold my breath
Referee, with the whistle, brrrrrt, hold his tech
Extendo clip, extendo roll
When your girl leave me, she need a hair salon
Hair weave killer going on a trapathon"

I smiled as one of the finest strippers I had ever seen walk on to stage dancing on my nigga. Duke nasty ass loved strippers; I'm surprised this nigga ain't gone broke from the amount of money he throws at them hoes.

I gotta give this bitch on stage props, she was highly recommended for private parties and I had to get the best for my nigga. The bitch surprised me when she flipped into the niggas lap putting her pussy all in his face, and this nigga grabbed her legs and ran his hands over her shit I had to laugh, he was drunk as fuck.

Once the song was over she kissed him on the cheek and he smacked her on her ass and she smiled and walked off stage. Duke came off stage staggering over to me grinning.

"Bro, that was one of the baddest strippers I ever seen." He said.

"Hell yeah, I ain't into them, but shawty definitely had talent," I said nodding.

"Hey Duke, happy birthday." I smiled because there was that beautiful voice again.

We both turned, and there was Noni and Lo. "Damn, Noni yo fine ass done grown up foreal, and Lo damn." He said licking lips.

"Aye, nigga chill on that one," I said mugging him.

He waved me off and grabbed each one of them into a hug. "I appreciate y'all coming thru." He slurred.

"Of course. I just wanted to personally say happy birthday before we head out." Noni said.

He nodded and hugged them again and then Noni looked at me before she turned and grabbed Lo and disappeared in to the crowd.

"Nigga you dumb as hell for letting Noni's attractive ass go." Instead of responding, I turned and walked away. I needed another drink. Halfway of me returning to VIP, someone grabbed my hand. I started to curse them out till I looked and seen it was Eve.

I looked her over, and she had on some tight ass blue dress barely covering her ass, and the heels she had on made her legs look ass thick and shit. I licked my lips and zeroed in on her breast before I looked at her.

"What's up ma?" I said.

"I've been looking for you." She whined, walking up on me running her hand down my chest.

I grabbed her hand and looked at her. "Oh yeah? What you looking for me for?"

"I was making sure you were leaving with me, Daddy." She snatched her hand away from me and ran it over my dick."

"Shit, you missed me huh." I said crossing my arms.

She bit her lip and looked at me nodding her head. "Follow me up to VIP, and you can roll out with me when I leave, and we can go to your house."

"Can't we go to your house? I've never been before." She pouted and leaned in trying to kiss me.

I quickly moved and looked at her like she was crazy. "Evelynn don't start that shit; you already know what's up. You're not my bitch, so you're not going to where I rest my head, and try that kissing shit again, and I'm going to break your fucking lips, now come on."

Not waiting for her to respond, I turned and continued my route to VIP and of course when I sat down she was right next to me. She sat on my lap, but she low key pissed me off, so I gently pushed her off me to the side and grabbed the blunt behind my ear and lit it. I looked up, and Sharee was standing there with her hands on her hips.

"Who is this Nike?" She asked.

"Are you my bitch?" I asked, before Eve could respond.

"No, but-"

"Exactly so don't fucking question me. Matter fact get the fuck up out of here you been killing my mood all night." I look over at security and motioned towards Sharee. He walked over and grabbed her.

"WHAT THE FUCK!" She yelled.

But he didn't respond he just continued dragging her out VIP, and she continued to yell.

"What the fuck was that?" Eve asked.

"Aye, you want to get dragged out next?" I asked raising my eyebrow and turning and looking at her. She didn't say anything else just crossed her arms and sat back, like I knew she would.

We partied till the club closed and once I made sure Duke and my sister were safely in the car. I stumbled over to Eve's car, and we headed to her house where I fucked her ass all night till be both passed out.

I called Trina to come get me early the next morning before Eve woke up so I can go home and shower and get a few hours of sleep in before we headed to Lo's house. Trina sent me a text saying she was outside. I made sure I had everything and hurried out Eve's apartment to Trina's car.

&

*T*rina and I got to Lo's house a little after three, and I knocked on the door and looked around. I don't know why I was so nervous. Maybe it was because I knew Noni low key hated me, after all, I done to her. But she was mine, and she needed to realize I changed and I wasn't that naïve kid I use to be anymore.

The door opened and a little boy appeared. "What do y'all want?" He asked staring at me.

"Jayceon I know yo ass didn't open my damn door," Lo said appearing and looking from us to the little boy.

"Sorry, mom." He said and took off running.

"Hey y'all, come in." She said moving to the side.

I let Trina walk in first and then I followed. She had a cute little ranch style home. We walked in and was right in the living room. It was nicely decorated in yellow and white with grey here and there. I looked around and wondered if Noni was staying here with her.

"Hey Trina girl, I swear it seems like I never see you even though we live in the same city," Lo said giving her a hug.

"I know, once your sister ditched me you did too," Trina pouted laughing.

"Girl bye, I didn't ditch you," Noni said coming from the back of the house.

She was wearing a wife beater and sweat pants, and I swear her ass grew even more then I thought last night.

"Best friend!" Trina yelled running over to her and jumping on her.

"Damn girl you acting like you missed me," Noni said laughing.

18

"Shut up, yo ass just up and disappeared and said fuck me because of my jackass brother."

Hearing Trina mention me caused Noni to look at me, like it clicked that I was in the room. Noni put on a fake smile, but you could tell it was forced. It killed me because I could see she still loved me, but I also could see the hurt I had caused her.

"Hey, King." She said finally making eye contact with me.

Before I could respond, a little boy came running into the room and up to her.

"Mommy, I'm hungry." He said.

Noni had a son, she left and went away and had a baby by another nigga. I stared at her trying to keep calm. I can't believe her ass had the nerve to go out and have a baby on me. Regardless of how I handled things with us, she was fucking mine, and I was the first to break that pussy in making it mine so she should have never let another nigga enter her, raw at that!

"You have a son?" I said finally finding my voice. I looked at Trina whose mouth was wide open looking from me to the little boy.

"Ye-ye-yes." She stuttered.

"So not only did you dip on a nigga, but you went and got fucking pregnant by someone!" I yelled, not really meaning too. I was pissed and hurt. I know I fucked up, but Noni knew I loved her, and it was just wrong timing with us in the past.

Her son jumped and clung to her legs before she picked him up. He dug his face into her neck and wrapped his arms around it.

"Noni, is there something you need to tell my brother?" Trina asked, looking from me to her."

But Noni didn't answer her instead she looked at me and was bouncing the little boy patting his back.

"Noni, it's time to come clean." Lo said.

But before she could reply to either of them, the little boy lifted his head and turned to look at me and I swear it was like looking in the mirror. The nigga she had a baby with was me.

CHAPTER 4

*N*oni
    I swear I just wanted to disappear and never come back. If looks could kill, I would be dead by the way King was looking at me.

"Noni, I swear your ass better start talking right now." He said looking at me through clenched teeth.

"Come on KJ let's go in the kitchen and get Trina, you, and Jayceon something to eat while mommy talks to her friend." Lo said.

But KJ clung to my neck. "Is he gonna hit you mommy?" He asked pulling back and looking at me.

I felt the tears forming in my eyes, but I wouldn't let them drop.

"Yo what the fuck did he just ask her?" King asked.

But I ignored him. "No baby go with auntie Lo while I talk to my friend okay. I'm fine." I kissed his cheek and handed him to Lo and they, along with Trina, headed to the kitchen.

I took a deep breath and walked over to the couch and sat down. I could feel King's eyes on me, but I couldn't look at him so I focused on my hands.

"Is he mine?" He asked.

"Yes." I said right above a whisper.

He laughed, but it wasn't a friendly laugh it was like he was trying to keep calm laugh.

"How old is he?"

"He's three, his name is Kingston Omar Tolliver Jr."

"So, I have a son, a three-year-old son and he's named after me, and I'm just now fucking finding out. Noni are you fucking serious?"

I don't know where the strength came from, but I jumped up and rush over to him and pointed my fingers at his chest.

"Don't fucking act like the first time I got pregnant you didn't tell me to have a fucking abortion and like a dumbass I listened to you. I went against what I believed to make you happy and got rid of my baby. So, no I wasn't giving you the chance to tell me to do it again."

"I was in fucking high school then Noni, I wasn't ready for a kid. The last time we had sex I was 22, I would have been more under-standing and open about it!"

"How was I to know that King? You betted on my fucking virginity and then had the nerve to have a girlfriend the whole time I thought we were building something and you demanded I had an abortion. Then when I run into you again I get drunk and sleep with you and end up pregnant again! I wasn't going through you rejecting me or my baby, so I left and went away for school and raised my son on my own!"

The tears I had tried to keep bottled in came pouring out. Saying it out loud, realizing the man I loved shitted on me so many times just for us to now share a kid together was too much for me.

He grabbed me and pulled me into his chest. "Your right, I'm sorry Noni, I didn't make this easy to deal with, but you should have told me. I have a son that knows nothing about me."

I sighed and pulled away from him.

"Do you want to meet him?" I asked.

"Hell yeah, but first why did he ask if I was gonna hit you?" I ignored him I didn't want to let him in on that part of my life, yet, so instead I called KJ into the room.

He came running to the room and jumped right into my arms. I kissed his cheeks and then turned and faced King.

"KJ, I have someone I want you to meet. Is that okay with you?" I looked at King and then back at our son, who slowly nodded his head.

I took a deep breath. "KJ, this is your dad, his name is Kingston too." I turned KJ more to face King.

"What's up little man?" He said attempting to reach for him, but KJ gripped my neck pulling away.

"So, I have two daddies, mommy?" He asked looking at me.

"I know he didn't just ask what I think he asked." King asked more to himself than to me.

"No, Deshawn was just your pretend dad. You know how you play make believe, but it's not real?" I asked, trying to get him to understand and King to relax.

He didn't answer me outloud. Instead he nodded his head.

"Well King is your real daddy, pretend is over." He slowly pulled away from me and looked at King again, and surprisingly he reached out for him. King slowly reached out and grabbed him, and KJ laid his head on his chest.

"Are you going to be nicer than my pretend daddy? He always made me and mommy cry." KJ asked.

Fuck, he just wouldn't stop. Instead of looking at King, I looked behind me, and sure enough, Lo and Trina were right there, with their nosy asses.

"Look here son, first and most importantly when you talk to someone always look them him the eyes, it shows respect." KJ slowly lifted his head and looked at him. "Secondly, I would never be mean to you and mommy, or make you cry on purpose."

I guess that was good enough because KJ was quiet after that. Trina walked over to us and stood in front of me with her hands on her hip.

I sighed and laughed a little. "KJ I have one more person for you to meet," I said, and he looked at me. But Trina took it upon herself to grab him out her brother's arms and introduce herself.

"What's up nephew, I'm your aunt, Trina." She said kissing his cheek, and it made him laugh. For some reason, his cheeks were ticklish as hell.

"Are you nicer than Aunt Lo? She always tells me no and puts me in time out." I laughed, Lo put KJ in time out one time, and his ass wouldn't let it go.

"Dang KJ foreal? Lo said walking up. I thought you loved me."

"I do, but you put me in timeout." He said folding his arms.

"Yes KJ, I'll be the cool aunt. She looked at Lo. How did you put this cute face in time out?" She began raining kisses on his cheeks again.

"Aye Trina chill out kissing all on my son like that damn, you gone make his ass soft," King said mugging her.

"Kingston shut up; I need to make up for lost times."

"Hey, you stole my name!" KJ said jumping out of Trina's lap and running up to King reaching for him again. I laughed because he acts like I didn't just tell him that.

"Nah little man you stole my name." He said picking him up and laughing. "I had it first."

"Are you and Aunt Trina going to stay forever?" He asked looking at King and then at Trina.

"Hell, yeah son, you and yo momma is stuck with us. And you have a grandma who's been bugging me for some grandkids. I'll take you to meet her too."

"Good because if Shawn comes to hurt mommy, you have to help her." He said and laid his head-on Kings chest and wrapped his arms around him.

The room grew silent, and I reached in my sweat pants, grabbed my phone and looked at the time. "Come on KJ it's time for you to take your nap," I said slowly walking over to him and Nike.

"But mom I want to hang out with my dad." He pouted never letting Nike go.

"You can hang out with him after your nap, come on so you can potty."

"No, I don't want to." He whined.

"Aye little man, you're not a baby or a girl." Nike said pulling him away and making him look at him. "You're a boy, and boys don't pout. Now your mom said it's time for a nap you say ok and go. We can hang out when you get up okay?"

He nodded his head and turned and looked at me. But Nike spoke to him again.

"And when someone asked you a question you open your mouth and speak. Got it?"

"Got it." He smiled and hugged Nike before reaching over to me. I smiled and kissed his cheek and turned and walked down the hall to get KJ ready for him nap.

"You know my momma is gonna be so mad at you right?" King asked me. Lo and I put the boys down for a nap, we decided to go sit on her deck with Trina and King to talk.

"I know I should have reached out to her and told her," I said taking a bite of my sandwich.

"Fuck that you should have told me! And who the fuck is Shawn and why is my son so fucking scared of him."

I didn't reply right away. I stared at my sandwich and then slowly looked up at King, whose eyes were piercing through me.

"Tell him Noni; he can't help if he doesn't know the whole story." I bit my lip and sighed.

"Shawn is my ex-boyfriend, I met him while I was going to school in Atlanta. After a year of us being together, he got abusive; it started off with a slap here and there but then the longer we were together, the worse he got. He never did it in front of KJ at first mainly when it was just me and him but after I caught him cheating and told him I was done he choked me and kicked me right in front of KJ when he was two."

I started to cry and looked down at my hands.

"I knew I had to leave but I only had one more year left of school, and I could leave Atlanta for good. So, I stayed, but he wouldn't leave me alone. He began yelling at KJ for little things and threatening him, and that's when I knew I had to leave. I didn't care what he did to me, but he wasn't touching my son. The night I heard this and confronted him he broke my nose, fractured my ribs, and threw KJ against the wall. So, once I left the hospital I left town, I moved an hour away and explained my situation to my professors and video chatted in the classes got my degree and came home."

"So, you were with this nigga for two fucking years letting him just beat your ass and puts his hands on my fucking son!" Nike yelled.

"King you don't understand I had a degree to get to make a future for my son. He was never like that to KJ until I caught him cheating. I would have left way before if that was the case."

"You should have brought your ass home and told me, and I would have been handled that nigga! Now you got my fucking son asking if I'm going to hurt him and shit!"

"Well maybe if you weren't such a fucking asshole in the first place I would have been comfortable telling you about KJ and coming to you for help!"

I wasn't about to argue with him, I got up and ran back into the house and in the room, I was staying in and slammed the door. I sat on the bed, and my mind drifted back to the night I got pregnant.

It was graduation night, and Trina was throwing a party at her brother's house to celebrate. Since I was leaving to go to Atlanta I decided to go, even though Nike was the last person I wanted to be around, I wasn't going to blow off my best friend's party.

I had on an all-white tank top and some khaki shorts that ended right below my ass cheek. My hair was thrown up in a slick ponytail, and I had on all white flip flops.

I walked in Nike's house, and smoke had instantly hit my face. I said hi to a few of my classmates and a couple of Nike's friends while making my way through the house trying to find Trina. I stopped by the bar and poured myself some the punch they had made when I felt a body behind me.

"Yo who told you to come out the house with all this ass hanging out." He whispered in my ear. I immediately felt my pussy get wet.

"Why are you so close to me Nike?" I said lightly pushing him away from me.

He grabbed me around my waist and began kissing my neck up to my ear.

25

"Quit playing with me Noni; you know the deal between us just like I do." He whispered again and this time bit my ear.

I had to put my drink down and grab the bar because my knees slightly buckled. I turned around and looked him in his face, and he took it upon his self to kiss me quickly and back away and winked at me before turning a walking away.

I laughed a little and shook my head and grabbed my drink and went back on my hunt to find Trina.

After finally finding Trina and four drinks later I was wasted. I was dancing and shaking my ass to every song that came on. And every dude that came up to me and tried to get behind me Nike shut down. He was really getting on my nerves.

I had snuck away and went and sat in Nike's room trying to sober up. If he was gonna keep ruining my fun I was leaving. I laid back on his bed and laid my arm over my face.

After a few minutes, I started to fall asleep, and I heard the door open. "Noni, you cool baby?" He asked.

"Nike, what do you want?" I groaned.

He chuckled. "Yo drunk ass is in my room in my bed. And don't call me Nike, you know I like when you say my real name."

"That's because you won't stop cock blocking my ass." I lifted my arm a little and looked at him.

He had on a black t-shirt and some basketball shorts. His hair was freshly cut, and the top had finally started getting some inches to it. I let my eyes roam down and looked down at his shorts and clenched my thighs together, remembering the day he took my virginity.

"Hell, yeah I'm cock blocking, you don't need to be with them niggas especially not in my house."

I laughed. "So, who do I need to be with King?"

He smiled and stood up and hovered over me and grabbed my shorts and began moving them down my thighs.

"King stop," I whined.

He reached up and lifted my shirt and began kissing on my stomach. I don't know if it was because I was drunk or because I truly loved this man, but my hormones went into overdrive soon as his lips touched my skin. I began running my hand through his hair. And he grabbed my shorts again and told me to raise up.

Once my shorts were off, and I was only in my panties he began kissing the outside down to my other lips.

"I'm sorry I hurt you Noni." He said in between kisses. But I didn't want to talk about that, so I ignored him.

He grabbed my panties and pulled them down and began French kissing my center, spreading it apart with his fingers flickering his tongue in and out.

"Fuck King." I moaned grabbing his hair again.

Slurp, lick, slurp, lick. Continuing pattern and I lost it once he stuck his finger in me.

"Cum for me Noni, show daddy you missed him." It was like my body was his slave and I came. He sucked my juices and began kissing up my body. He slowly removed my bra and hovered me. I looked at him as if I was hypnotized. He leaned down and began kissing me parting my lips with his tongue.

I welcomed his tongue in my mouth and began to suck on it, and somewhere in between this he managed to get his shorts and boxers off and thrust himself inside me.

I gripped the back of his neck, and he pulled back looking at me going in and out of me slowly.

"I know I fucked up Noni, and I can admit that. But you know I love you. You love me still, don't you?" I felt tears fill my eyes and I felt him stop.

"You love me, don't you?" He asked again staring at me intensely.

"Yes, King I love you." He smiled and buried his face into the crook of my neck and began planting soft kisses on it.

His thrusts began to speed up, and my body instantly reacted and started meeting his stroke.

"I'm about to cum again King!" I yelled.

"Me too, cum with me baby." He crashed his lips into mine, and a felt my body began to shake and he crashed on me.

I laid there not saying anything, and he got up grabbed his clothes and got off the bed and went into the bathroom connected to his room.

I hurried and got dressed and rushed out the room, sobering up fast. I ran out the house and to my car and began crying soon as I closed my car door. I *texted Trina and told her I was heading home and made a promise to myself I would never be a fool to Kingston Tolliver again.*

I sat with my head in my hands and silently cried. I hated I was so weak over a man but I loved him, and it wouldn't go away. There was a slight knock on my door and it open and in walked King, why couldn't he just leave me alone.

CHAPTER 5

*N*ike

Hearing Noni admit what that nigga did to her, and my son had me ready to put a bullet through his head. I know it was my fault why Noni ran and was so against telling me about KJ and maybe her running clouded her thought process, but she had to know if she wanted to keep KJ then I would have been there.

We all sat there silently in our thoughts. I'm sure all thinking about what Noni had just revealed.

"Go talk to her Nike." Trina said. "You guys have a kid that you need to worry about. It's time for you both to grow up and work this out."

She was right, but how was I going to fix this. I ran my hand through my hair before getting up.

"Her room's the last door in the back of the hallway," Lo said. I nodded and walked in and checked on my son first.

I smiled looking at him; he was curled up mouth open knocked out. I can't believe I missed three years of his life. I lightly closed the door and shook my head. Trina was right I had to fix this.

I got to the door and took a deep breath and knocked and opened the door. She looked up at me with red swollen eyes.

I closed the door behind me and walked over to the bed and sat down and pulled her into my chest.

I held her as she cried and the more she did the worse I felt. I could have prevented this.

"Noni, please stop crying, you know I hate that shit man," I said rubbing her back.

"I'm sorry I kept him from you, King, I just didn't know what to do. I didn't know I was pregnant until I got to Atlanta and I was scared, but I knew I couldn't go through that procedure again."

I took a deep breath. "I should have never made you go through it the first time. I should have manned up and taken care of my responsibilities. I'm happy you kept this one though, he seems like a good kid."

"Yeah, he is, he acts just like you though. I swear he's the smoothest talking three-year-old I've ever seen." She wiped her eyes and laughed.

I thought back to when I made that dumbass bet. I really did care for Noni, she was always at my house with Trina and watching her grow up and seeing how cool and down to earth she was made me fall in love with her. That bet actually made it easier to show it because everyone thought I was just acting and just trying to get in her pants but I enjoyed being around her.

"I hate that I missed so much and even though I should be pissed at you I understand why you did what you did. But I need to know about this nigga who put his hands on you and my son?"

"I don't want to talk about that right now; I just want to know how we're going to fix this."

"Noni, you got me fucked up. Do you think you can tell me some shit like that and I just brush it off?"

"No, but I also want you to focus on getting to know your son. I promise I'll tell you everything and I want Deshawn to get what he deserves, but right now I want you to just get to know KJ."

"And what about us?"

"What about us? There is no us; we have a son."

"I want us to be together as a family Noni."

She pulled away from me and looked at me. "Look, King, it's been too much that has gone on between us. I don't want to be with you on that level, every time I opened up to you; you shitted on me."

I chuckled slightly. Noni was lying to me and herself. I know I fucked up, but I know that Noni is it for me and I was going to make her believe me no matter what I had to do."

I stood up, turned, grabbed her hands and pulled her up and into me. I hugged her tightly and kissed the top of her head. I pulled back and lifted her chin and crashed my lips into hers, when she didn't pull back I parted her lips with my tongue.

I moved my hands down into her sweat pants and pulled on them. She gripped my hands, but didn't pull back. I grabbed her hand and moved it out the way and pushed my hand down her pants and her ass didn't have on panties!

I parted her lower lips with my finger and pushed one inside of her stroking her in and out. I pulled my mouth away from her and bent down and began kissing her neck. I took my thumb and began rubbing on her clit while sticking another finger in her.

"Fuck King, baby." She moaned.

"Let it go baby, make it rain on daddy." I whispered in her ear.

She grabbed my waist and her body began to shake and my hand became drenched.

I slowly pulled my hand out her sweat panties and stuck each finger in my mouth.

"Your still sweet as fuck." I looked at her and she was trying to get her breathing together.

I began to kiss her again and attempted to take her shirt off but she stopped me. "No King, we can't do this. I can't take it there with you again."

"Noni, I'm ready for this. I know I fucked up in the past, but it'll be different. I just need you to have faith in me."

"King I can't, I'm sorry but I've heard this too many times from you. I have no problem with you being in our son's life but that's all it'll be."

She pulled away from me and started towards the door. It was like every step she took broke me more and more.

"Noni!" I yelled when she reached for the doorknob.

She stopped and turned and faced me again. The look on her face broke my heart and the tears rolling down her cheeks killed me. I slowly walked over to her and grabbed her.

"I'm going to give you space for now, I know that it's hard to trust me with my track record but I'm going to show you this is what I want. I love you." I kissed her forehead and stepped back and watched her walk out the door.

I couldn't believe I had a son that I knew nothing about and it was my fault. I remember Noni coming to me a few months after I took her virginity telling me she was pregnant and I laughed in her face and convinced her that a baby was something we didn't need. She cried and begged me to be ok with her keeping it, but I made it known she was going to be a single parent because I didn't want a kid then.

Looking back now I was stupid as fuck. Noni was a great catch, and I feel like all the pain she's been through over the last couple years was because of me. If I would have never treated her how I did, then she would have never moved and thought being with that fuck boy was ok, and my son would have been known me.

I shook my head and went into my pocket and grabbed my vibrating phone. I looked, and it was Eve. I know she was probably calling to complain because I dipped on her ass this morning, but I had more important shit to worry about than dealing with her annoying ass.

I took a deep breath and headed out the door and walked back into the living room. I looked at Trina and Noni in the living room talking, and instead of disturbing them I walked into the kitchen and seen Lo, in the fridge.

"How do I fix this?" I asked.

She jumped and turned around. "God, Nike you scared the fuck out of me!"

I laughed. "I'm sorry, but I need your help." She stared at me for a minute then headed toward the back door.

I turned following behind her. We went back outside to the patio, and she sat in one of the chairs, and I sat down across from her. She didn't speak at first instead she just stared at me.

"Look, Nike, I'm rooting for you I really am, in fact, my nephew deserves to be in a two-parent home." She started.

"So how do I make that happen?"

"You fucked up, like not only did you play her but you treated her like some random ass jump off. We both know Noni isn't the one for games, so the fact that this happened twice isn't going to make this easy."

"I know man, but I was young at the time and being in something serious wasn't what I wanted. But Noni is it for me, I know I fucked up with the bet and abortion, and I regret that shit every day."

She didn't say anything. Instead, she stared at me. "Abortion? What abortion?"

"She didn't tell you?" She shook her head. "Hell no, what are you talking about?" I ran my hand down my face and sighed.

"When we were in high school after I took her virginity, she found out she was pregnant. She called me one day asking me to meet her, and when I did, she told me the news. I didn't believe her, so we went to a store and got a test, and we went back to my house, and she took it right in front of me, and it came back positive."

I took a deep breath, going over this and saying it out loud was really showing me how fucked up I was.

"So how did an abortion come into play?" She asked.

"I told her I wasn't ready for a kid, I was 17 about to be 18, and I was wild as fuck in high school, so a kid just didn't fit into the equation for me at the time. She cried and begged me to be ok with her keeping it, and I kept telling her basically she was gonna be a single parent because I didn't want it. A week later she found out about the bet, and following that she texted me and told me it was done."

"You're shitting me, right? She was only 14, and you made her have an abortion? No wonder why she doesn't want to give you another try."

"I know, it was fucked up, at the time I meant it but if I could go back, I wouldn't have done that. I'm happy she kept KJ though, I'm excited to get to know my little nigga."

My phone got to ringing before Lo could respond, I looked at it and ignored it again. I was gone smack the fuck out of Eve's dumb ass if she didn't stop blowing up my phone.

"Look, Noni loves you, but you hurt her and now that I know everything I don't blame her. If you really want her back just give her space, be there for KJ and let her get her emotions in check."

"Man, but what if she doesn't want me back. I swear to God if I feel like she's trying to fuck with another nigga I'm killing him no questions asked."

She laughed and looked at me. She had no idea how serious I was, that nigga Deshawn already had a bullet with his name on it and soon as I found out where that nigga be at it's over.

"Just give it time, seeing you again brought out a lot of emotions in her so just let her handle that before you try anything."

I didn't say anything back; I just nodded my head a stood up and walked towards the door. I was gonna spend a little time with my son and then leave. I'd give Noni some space, but she had me fucked up if she thought it was gonna be for a long time.

CHAPTER 6

Trina

Do Not Answer: So, you gone stop by the crib so we can talk about last night?

I looked at the text message I had just received and relocked my phone. That was problems I didn't need or want to deal with right now.

"Trina, are you listening to me?" Noni asked.

"Yeah, girl my bad, what did you say?" I asked.

"I asked what's been going on since I last seen you."

"Girl nothing, trying to figure my life out. I laughed. I finished school and got a degree in early childhood development, with a minor in psychology, and now I just need to figure out where I want to take it."

"I thought you wanted to be a youth counselor?"

My phone went off again, and I glanced at it.

Do Not Answer: You gone leave me on read? Cool, I'll be seeing you.

I laughed but didn't open this message and looked back at Noni who was side eyeing me.

"Bitch who is that?" She said.

"Who is who?"

"The person yo ass is ignoring."

"Girl just some nigga I hooked up with and won't leave me alone." I laughed. "But in seriousness, I do want to the counselor thing, but I want to start my own center I don't want to work for anybody."

"Girl, then do it what's stopping you." I really didn't have an answer, so instead, I shrugged my shoulders.

"Anyways, bitch how are you not going to tell me you had a whole ass baby by my brother?" I whispered and looked behind to make sure Nike wasn't around.

She shrugged. "I didn't want him to know honestly. After I had that abortion, my spirits were crushed, and I just felt like this was God giving me a second chance and I refused to let your brother ruin that."

"I told your ass then not get it, fuck what my brother was talking about."

"I know, but I loved his ugly ass, so I did it to make him happy." She stopped and wiped her eyes. "I just look at KJ every day and remember that day and sometimes I have to stop myself from crying about it. I really want to hate your brother, but I shouldn't have gone through with it."

I scooted over closer to her and wrapped my arms around her. "KJ is here now, and maybe at the time, it wasn't meant for you to have a baby. You were a sophomore turning 15, and you were one best sprinters our track team had. Did you really want to be a mom then?"

"No, but it was my baby, I don't even believe in abortions, I only did it to make King happy."

"I shouldn't have made you make that decision."

I turned around and seen Nike standing there with his hands in his pockets.

"Look I got some stuff to take care of, and you two need to talk at least come to an agreement for my nephew's sake. I turned back to Noni and pulled away. Let's go to the mall tomorrow or something, so I can bond with KJ."

She didn't say anything only nodded. I got up and hugged her and walked behind the couch and hugged my brother. "Fix this," I whispered and kissed his cheek.

I walked towards the door. "Tell Lo I said I'll see her later. I said and headed out.

I walked to my car and hopped in and headed towards my house. While driving, I took a minute to reflect what happened. My ass got too drunk after Duke's party and fucked up big time, that's why I didn't drink.

I shook my head as I pulled into my driveway seeing the car that was waiting for me.

I got out and ignored him and walked to my door. "So, you don't see me fucking sitting here?" He asked, and I heard his door slam.

I rolled my eyes and unlocked my door and walked in, leaving it open for him to come in. Once I heard my front door close, I turned and looked at him.

I had never looked at him differently until now, but he was fine as fuck. He was light skinned, with gray, green eyes depending on the light, 6'2 and about 200 pounds. He wasn't cut like my brother but he was still fit, he had a Caesar haircut with as many waves as the ocean from brushing it all the time. He didn't have a lot of facial hair, only a mustache and a little bush on his chin. His lips were bright pink, how I didn't know with all the weed he smoked, but they were big a juicy and fit his face perfectly. He wasn't covered in tattoos on his arms, but his chest and back were.

"Duke, I don't know what you want me to say." I sighed and crossed my arms and leaned to the side.

"Trina, we fucked last night. Your brother is my best friend, and you're like my little sister. I just want to make sure we straight I don't want it to be awkward." He said shrugging his shoulders.

"You're making it that way. We were both drunk, and we fucked up. Nike doesn't have to know, and it can stay between us. Besides I barely remember it anyway."

He stared at me for seconds, chuckled and put his hands in his pocket. "You don't remember it huh?"

I slowly shook my head. "No, I was fucked up. Now if that was all I'm about to take a nap."

"You got something to eat?" He asked.

I rolled my eyes and turned to walk towards my room. "You and Nike need to find yall a woman. There's leftover roast in the fridge."

I started walking towards my room and didn't wait for him to reply. I opened my door and shut it and immediately stripped out my clothes and got on top of my comforter.

I took my panties off, they were soaked. Okay, I lied I remembered everything about last night. Duke took my body to places I didn't even know existed, and that nigga ate the fuck out my pussy. Even though I know we should have never taken it there I got to admit, I see why he has bitches acting crazy about him.

I got up and walked to the end of my bed and grabbed my phone out of my pocket and started surfing through social media but that wasn't distracting me enough. I put my phone on my night stand and laid down and started rubbing my clit. I inserted a finger remembering Duke's performance last night. I closed my eyes and began working on my lower half feeling myself getting hotter. I began rubbing on my breast with my other hand and just when I was almost there my door opened, and my eyes popped open.

"Aye Trina, I'm about to head out," Duke said as he opened the door.

"Duke what the fuck, you don't know how to knock in someone's house." He didn't answer. Instead he walked in and shut the door.

"What you doing Trina?"

"What does it look like? I was trying to cum before you interrupted me." He chuckled a little and bit his lip.

"Get the fuck out!" I yelled.

But instead of listening he walked closer to the bed, laid on it, grabbed ankles and pulled me towards him.

"You said you don't remember last night huh?" He asked, slowly brushing his fingers over my clit.

"Duke no, now stop." I moaned. He laughed again and stuck his finger in me.

"Damn that's a shame because I remember your shit, the way yo pussy was gripping my shit and wetting me up." He leaned down and kissed the top of my pussy.

"Duke please." I looked down at him.

"Please what Trina?" He said with a smirk and kissed my pussy this time. I leaned up on my elbows and looked him in his eyes.

"Eat my pussy please," I begged. Fuck it we had already crossed that line, and I needed this.

He didn't say anything, and I felt his tongue run over my pussy, and he began sucking on it pulling it in his mouth.

"Shit Duke." I moaned low and closed my eyes and arched my back.

He inserted his finger in me and started sucking on my pussy harder. "Duke, I can't take it," I said trying to pull away. He gripped my legs locking me in place.

"Let that shit go baby. Quit playing." He said in my pussy, and that's all I needed to hear.

Instead of him stopping he kept kissing and sucking and finally pulled up. I opened my eyes and looked at him and seen my juices in his chin hair. I bit my lip and looked down at his basketball shorts and seen his imprint standing. I pushed myself off the bed and crawled down to the end of the bed where he stood up. I got on my knees.

"I wanna taste myself." I said. He stuck his tongue out, and I pulled it into my mouth and began sucking on it. I ran my hand down his chest and put it in his shorts and grabbed his dick and began stroking it. I pulled away from him and looked him in the eye.

I saw the lust he had for me and him biting his lip turned me on even more. I began kissing his neck, and he grabbed my wrist that was in his pants.

"Trina if you don't chill, I'm going to push you face down in yo bed and fuck the shit out of you." He said.

I pulled away from him and smiled. I turned around and got on my hands and knees and arched my back. "You mean like this?"

When I didn't hear him answer, I turned, and I saw he now had his dick in his hand and was stroking his dick slowly.

"Grab your ass cheeks and spread them, I wanna see that pussy." He said, in a sexy ass raspy voice. Doing what I was told I spread my ass cheeks and felt my bed dip.

"This got to be the last time we do this Trina." He said. I didn't answer him. I knew he was right, but instead of responding I wanted him in me.

He slapped my ass. "Do you hear me?"

"Yes, now please put it in."

Once again, he went silent. Just when I was about to say something again, I felt him shove his dick in me and I swear my breath was taken away. Duke was working with at least 9 inches of thick dick.

"Arch that back more!" He said smacking my ass again. I did what he told me and released my ass cheeks and gripped the sheets.

"Now come on Trina, throw that ass back like you were last night. You don't remember, right? I'm about to refresh shit for you."

"Duke, fuck," I yelled and started throwing it back.

"Shit Trina why the fuck yo pussy so tight." He gripped my hair and pulled me up to him and put his chest against my back and reached around me and started playing with my clit.

He started kissing on my neck, and I swear I felt like I was finna explode. "You still don't remember?" He whispered in my ear before biting it.

"I remember! I yelled. I'm about to cum Duke, fuck!" He slowed his strokes and began hitting me long and hard. I swear I came so hard I felt like this nigga took my whole soul with him.

He pulled out of me and got on the side of me and laid down on his back and grabbed me.

"Get on top." He demanded me. "I'm tired," I whined. He ain't give a fuck; he pulled me on top of him anyway. I rolled my eyes and slowly sat on him.

I begin bouncing up and down, and he sat up and took one of my nipples in his mouth and sucked on it. I threw my head back and began to bounce faster. My nipples have always been one of my spots

"That's right baby, show daddy you can handle this dick." He said taking my other breast in his mouth.

"Duke bite my nipple," I yelled. He did as I asked and gently began nibbling on my nipple. He pulled away and looked at me, and I leaned down and kissed him. He stuck his tongue in my mouth and smacked my ass. I pulled away and twisted my body and began riding him reverse cowgirl and grabbed his thighs.

"Damn Trina, you doing it like that," I smirked when I felt him beginning to match my bounce.

"Duke, I'm about to come again," I yelled. "Fuck me too!" After a few minutes, my whole body shook, and I felt Duke tense up, and I fell to the side.

"Fuck man, yo ass got a nigga stuck and shit." I laughed and pulled my leg from around him and turned and looked at him.

I looked down and frowned. "Duke I forgot your ass didn't have a condom on," I said.

"You're on birth control, right?" He asked.

"Yeah but that's not the point."

"Shit Trina, I felt that shit without a glove last night, and there was no way I was putting one on today. Plus, you know me I don't go in bitches raw, so I'm clean." I rolled my eyes and laid down.

I felt him get up and seen him walk around the bed towards the connecting bathroom. I heard him go into the cabinets and then I heard the water running. He then walked into the room and sat on the bed and tapped me on my legs.

"Open your legs." I slowly opened them, and he ran a wash cloth between. He got up and went back into the bathroom, and I stared at his beautiful third leg. He came back into the room and looked at me and grabbed his boxers and shorts put them on and sat on the bed.

"Trina, you know yo brother can't find out, right?" I rolled over and sat up.

"Duke I know, his ass would kill us if he found this out."

"We can't do this again either. I fucked up walking in on you, and I shouldn't have taken it there again."

"Look we shouldn't have done it, but we're both grown so fuck it," I said shrugging shoulders. He laughed and shook his head.

"Come lock the door big head." He raised off the bed. I got off the bed and walked over to my closet and grabbed my robe and followed him out my room and to the front door.

He got to the door and grabbed the knob but turned and looked at me instead of opening it. He leaned down and pecked my lips and few times before fully kissing me and grabbing my waist. He pulled me into him and grabbed my ass. I wrapped my arms around him and stuck my tongue in his mouth.

After a few minutes, he pulled away from me and wiped his mouth. "Shit I'm fucking up." He said, and a shook his head. "Bye Trina."

This time he turned and opened the door and walked out. I smiled about locked the door and headed to my room and to shower and finally fall asleep.

I had never looked at Duke as more than a brother and even though I know, we shouldn't, I already felt myself addicted to him. I just hope I can fight my urges for him.

CHAPTER 7

$\mathcal{D}$uke
One month later

Damn man, I was really fucking up. I pulled into my house and got out and walked up to my door and unlocked it and walked in.

I know I shouldn't have been thinking about her, but Trina's ass was on my mind like crazy. I had fucked a few bitches since my birthday, and I swear none of they shit gripped my dick like her pussy did.

"FUCK! I yelled. I knew Trina was off limits. Nike didn't play about Trina, that was like his daughter always been like that. I hadn't seen that nigga foreal, and that was good I don't know if I could look at him knowing I had smashed his sister. He's been bonding with his son and shit. I can't believe my nigga was a father, Noni was good for him, so hopefully, he got his shit together.

I walked into my house and down the hall and walked into my bedroom and stripped down to my boxers. I climbed into my bed and put my hands behind my head and closed my eyes.

Trina's pretty ass kept popping up, her slim ass body she wasn't stacked or anything, but she had a nice size ass for her size and a nice set of boobs, they weren't huge, but they weren't small, just big enough to take a handful of. Her red shoulder length hair complimented her cinnamon brown skin, and her smile was bright as fuck. She was 5'4 about 135 lbs. Trina was in a league of her own, she had her own style that fit her personality, you couldn't help but fall for her.

I had fallen asleep with Trina on my mind and had a wet dream about her ass. I felt her mouth wrapped around my dick and jerking me off the same time. "Fuck Trina suck that dick baby." I moved my hands down, and my eyes shot open when I felt hair.

"Trina, what the fuck!" I yelled trying to pull her up, and she smacked my hands away and began playing with my balls.

"Fuck, what the fuck!" I yelled. I grabbed her hair and began moving her head up on down. "Put it all in your mouth baby," I said.

I continued humping her face, and she took more of me into her mouth. She gagged a little, pulled back, spit on my dick and began running her hand up and down it before putting it back in her mouth.

"Trina, pull up I'm about to come." I went to pull her up, and she smacked my hands away again and looked at me, and I shot my load in her mouth.

She sucked me dry and pulled away and hopped up and went into the bathroom, I heard her gargle and spit, and she came back out a few minutes later.

"Trina, what are you doing here?" I asked. She didn't answer me. Instead she climbed on the bed and crawled over me and started kissing me and stroking my dick.

"I just need you to fuck me one more time; I promise after this I'll be good." She whispered in my ear. I sighed feeling my dick grow in her hands. I grabbed her hips and flipped her over and hovered over here.

"Trina this has to be the last time. I said looking at her. She nodded her head and grabbed my dick and pulled it towards her entrance. I grabbed my dick from her and began rubbing it against her pussy. She was wet as fuck; I never fucked a bitch that soaked my shit like her little ass. I slapped my dick against her pussy, and she moaned.

"Duke, please come on!" She said. I chuckled a little and plunged my dick into her. "This what you wanted huh," I said leaning down and taking her breast in my mouth.

"Yes baby, fuck me." I took my dick out leaving the tip in and pushed it back in. I repeated that a few more times and began rolling my hips, and her ass started matching my thrust.

"Trina, I swear yo ass is trouble. You ain't been fucking since last time, have you?" I asked.

Her shit was squeezing the fuck out my dick; it was no way she been fucking anyone else. I had to think of random shit to keep from busting.

"No daddy, it' been waiting for you." She moaned. Fuck why did she say that? I leaned down and kissed her and started moving my hips faster and harder.

"I'm about to cum Duke!" She yelled. "Me too baby, cum with me." I thrust into her harder, and my body jerked, and I shot my seeds into her. I fell forward on her and laid on her chest. I ran my tongue over her nipple, and she let out a sexy ass moan, and my dick rose again. If this was foreal going to be the last time then we were going to go a few rounds I thought as I sat up and turned her on her stomach.

After Trina left and be both agreed that we had to stop I got a call from Nike to meet him at his mom's house. I loved Nike's mom she took care of me as if I was her own. My mom died when I was in 3rd grade from breast cancer, that's actually how me and Nike became cool.

I was angry after my mom died and used to act up in school. These 4th graders use to pick with me because I came to school crying so I punched one of them at recess and his two friends ain't like that, so they tried to jump me, and Nike came out of nowhere and helped me and beat the nigga's asses and got suspended too. That day forward that was my nigga and no one fucked with us.

Nike saved my ass a few times. Since my mom died, I became short tempered as fuck. My dad was my nigga and tried to talk to me, and even my step mom tried to be there for me, but I never got over my mom dying. I was a momma's boy, I ain't afraid to admit it, so I use to just do dumb shit. Even till this day, it's been plenty times Nike had to talk me out of doing dumb shit that might end with me in jail. I've been told I needed to talk to someone, but they had me fucked up.

I was thankful Nike's mom took me in though, I spent more time at their house than I did at mines. My dad worked a lot so he was hardly home once I could watch myself. Momma T, always told me I was always welcomed, her and Nike's dad became my second parents, and I'd forever be grateful. That's why I feel so bad about Trina, I watched her ass grow up, and now I was fucking her.

I pulled into Nike's parents' house and parked next to his car and got out and walked up to the door and pushed it open. I walked straight back to the kitchen because I smelled food and I know if she was cooking that's where Nike was.

"What's up family?" I said walking into the kitchen. I walked behind Momma T and kissed her cheek.

"Hey, baby." She said.

I walked up to Nike and slapped hands with him. I looked at him and shook my head looking KJ sitting next to him.

"Man, this little nigga looks just like you." I said.

"I know, Noni must have really hated my ass during her pregnancy." He said laughing.

"Kingston watch your mouth! Especially in front of my baby." Momma T said turning and looking at him.

"My bad ma." He said throwing his hands.

"What's up little man." I said rubbing my hand over his head.

He laughed. "What's up Unc."

"Man, he sounds just like you." I said looking at Nike.

"I know, Noni so mad, he connected with me so quick he doesn't want to leave me half the time."

"Speaking of Noni, I hope she's coming over today because her little ass been dodging me since she's been back." Momma T said.

Nike and I laughed. "Yeah, she's coming with Trina." As if on cue we heard the front door open and Noni and Trina walked in the kitchen a few seconds later.

"Hey yall," Trina said and leaned down and kissed KJ.

"Mommy!" He yelled and jumped out the chair and ran over to Noni and she picked him up and kissed his cheek.

"Hey, baby. Hey everyone." She said.

"Uh huh, Noni come over and give me a hug, and then everyone go into the dining room so we can sit now and eat." She put KJ and slowly walked over to Momma T and hugged her.

"Where's daddy?" Trina asked.

"He won't be back till tomorrow," Nike said and grabbed KJ and headed into the dining room and we followed.

We all sat down, and a few seconds later Noni and Momma T came in with pans and sat down. We said grace and dug in.

Once we were done Momma T took KJ into the living room to watch TV so we could talk, well her and Noni, we were just being nosey.

"Now Noni you know you're on my shit list, right?" She said looking at her. She slowly shook her head up and down.

"I know Momma T; I just was in a bad place with King when I got pregnant I really didn't think of anyone else. I found out I was pregnant my second month I was in school, and I just didn't see the need to disrupt King's life."

"Disrupt my life? Nike said looking at her. That's my whole ass son."

She ignored him and continued talking to Momma T.

"I know it hurts you guys and it sucks KJ missed the first three years of his life without you guys, and I'm sorry, but at the time I thought I was doing what was best for him."

"Bullshit, you were being selfish as fuck!" Nike yelled making her jump.

"Kingston stop yelling at that girl and look what you put her through." Momma T said.

"And what about me. I fucked up with her and I know that, but she kept my fucking son away from me and had some fuck nigga beating her ass and raising my fucking seed. Y'all got me fucked up." He got up and stormed into out the dining room towards the living room. I looked over, and Noni was crying.

"I'll talk to him," I said and got up and headed after Nike. I walked into the living room, and he was sitting next to KJ.

"Bro, come outside with me really quick," I said nodding towards the door. He nodded and walked over to the door. I walked out after him, walked to my car and opened the door and grabbed the half smoked blunt out my ash tray. I reached into my pocket and pulled out my lighter and lit and walked over to him and handed it over.

I didn't say anything; I waited until he was ready. "Noni really fucked me up man. I know I fucked up, but she kept my whole son from me and my family for three years, and everyone thinks that I'm supposed to overlook that."

He passed the blunt back to me. "Look bro I'm not gonna say I understand what you're going through because I don't. I started. Your right you fucked up, but that's no reason to keep your kid from you. I love Noni like a sister but she fucked up too, but you can't blow up like that she was scared as fuck when you yelled."

He ran his hands through his hair and sighed. "I know man, Noni the only one that can make me lose my cool that quick man. It's like I want to be with her and be a family, shit knock her ass up again hopefully with a little girl, but the other part of me is so pissed she did some shit like this."

I laughed at his ass and passed the blunt. "Look yall need to talk, yall both obviously got stuff to talk about and if you want to be with her yall need to put everything on the table."

"Man, I can barely get her to talk to me. If it don't got to do with KJ, she won't talk to me. I moved her and KJ into they own spot because I wanted him to have his own stuff you know and she cursed me out. He laughed and shook his head.

I just can't win, she thinks I'm trying to buy myself into her life. I just don't understand why if I have the money and her and my son need a place to live why it's a problem."

"Man, you know Noni's is independent as fuck, she always been," I said laughing.

"You right about that. I just need her to talk to me, and I'll be good."

48

I didn't comment back because he knew how Noni was and she wasn't talking until she was ready. We finished the blunt and went back into the house. KJ had fallen asleep so we went back into the dining room and all three women looked at us.

Nike walked over to his mom and kissed her and cheek then over to Noni and did the same thing and apologized.

It was an awkward silence. "So, what was y'all talking about," I asked.

"Nothing," Trina said quickly. Her mom waved her off. "I'm trying to get Trina to tell me who's been blowing her back out."

I choked and looked at Trina. "Mom, what the hell, I don't want to hear that shit," Nike said.

"Kingston watch your damn mouth. Plus, I just wanted to know. My baby is glowing and whoever he is must be hung my baby finally getting some thickness to her."

"MOM!" Both Trina and Nike yelled. "What we all grown." She said shrugging her shoulders.

"It's nobody important. Just a guy I talk to here and there."

"Well do I know him?" Noni asked.

"No, I went to school with him. Look can we talk about something else."

"If you serious with this nigga then I need to meet him, me and Duke need to make sure he ain't no fuck nigga."

"Oh, trust me I'm sure yall would love him. He reminds me a lot of Duke actually." She looked directly at me and smirked.

Nike started laughed. "Then hell no, if he acts like Duke that means he's fucking a lot of bitches and don't give a fuck whose feelings he hurt." That dropped the smile off her face.

"I didn't say he was like him in that way I just meant personality."

"Aye Nike we got to meet up with Cortez at the warehouse," I said breaking up they debate.

"Shit I forgot about that, come on I'll drive." Even though Nike had left the drug game alone, he came to our meetings once a month, he was like a silent partner. We got up and kissed the girls on the cheeks, and Trina rubbed her hand over dick. I jumped back and looked at her, and she winked and smiled. I looked around, and no one was paying us any attention. I shook my head and walked out the dining room after saying bye to everyone.

My mind was stuck on Trina's ass so bad that I didn't even realize that we had pulled into the warehouse.

"Duke nigga you cool?" Nike asked.

I didn't respond at first. Instead, I laughed to myself because I was definitely tripping. Trina was like my sister, and I had fucked her more than once. The bad part is I enjoyed it, and I wanted to continue it, but I knew Nike would never be okay with it.

Shit if Trina were my sister I wouldn't want her with anyone like me either. I dogged out bitches left and right with her brother. Shit, it's been times we fucked the same bitch and sent her on her way. I have only been in one serious relationship, and that was in high school shit, and even then, I couldn't stay faithful, so I knew me getting too involved with Trina wouldn't be good.

"Duke!" Nike yelled my name this time.

"Shit my bad, I was thinking about some shit," I said reaching for the handle.

"Aye, what the fuck is up with you? You been doing that shit a lot lately."

"Nigga I'm cool, let's go." This time I opened the door and got out.

I know I had to do something to keep Trina off my mind, but the way her pussy gripped my dick and she sucked my shit had me wanting to go buy her ass a ring ass marry her right on the spot. SHIT!

I hurried and focused my thoughts elsewhere and adjusted myself; there was no way I was walking in this room full of niggas with a hard as dick. Trina was definitely fucking up my mental and I needed to fix it ASAP.

CHAPTER 8

$\mathcal{E}$velynn

    I can't believe it's been a month since I talked to Nike! I've called and texted him, and he's been straight ignoring me. Ever since that bitch Shonni came back he acts like I don't exist. It's been a little over a year since I've been dealing with him and he still treats me like some jump off bitch.

I've never been to his house, and he never even tries to take me out, but all that's finna change. I followed him one day from his shop to his house, and so I figured I'll just pop up on him and make him talk to me.

I had just pulled up to his house, and I can't lie I thought he would live in something way flashier. This was a two story, beige color house. It was a decent size, something I could see our kids running around in when we had them.

I got parked and got out the car and tugged on my dress I had on. He wasn't gonna resist me in this Nike loved my body.

I walked up to the house and looked around. I saw a white Civic in the driveway, and I know for a fact it wasn't his. He better have not had another bitch here.

I stalked up and the door and began banging on it.

"Nike open the fucking door! I yelled. And if you got a bitch in there with you I'm beating her ass!"

I continued to bang on the door and finally heard the locks twist. The door opened, and some bitch answered. I stared at her in her shorts and tank top before I pushed past her.

"Who the fuck are you? And why the fuck are you banging on me door!" She yelled.

I ignored her and began speed walking going further in the house until I was yanked back.

"What the fuck are you doing? Get the fuck out!"

"Where the fuck is Nike?" NIKE! I yelled.

"Nike doesn't live here."

"Bitch don't lie I seen him come to this house a few times and he has a key so where the fuck is he!" I tried to walk towards the back again, and she grabbed me again and pushed me this time. I stumbled at first out of reflex I swung and hit her once I caught myself. What I didn't see is the two piece she was gonna send my way.

Next thing I know we were going back to back hitting and she stopped when a little boy came out yelling for me.

"Mommy!" He yelled.

She stopped and looked, and I took the opportunity and pushed her, and she fell backward and I hopped on her connecting my fist to her, but she grabbed my hair and yanked head down.

At this point I didn't even care about Nike being here I was mad this bitch got some good shots in on me.

"Bitch get the fuck off me!" She yelled.

I felt little fist hitting me and yelling for me to get off their mom but I was so in the zone that I pushed him off me before I could stop myself.

"Bitch!" She yelled and flipped me over and stood up and ran over to her little bastard son.

I looked over, and he was laying down not moving, and I realized he hit his head on one of her tables.

"Fuck I'm sorry! I was just looking for Nike!" I said standing up.

"Bitch, when he finds out you did this to his son he's gonna fucking kill you!" She said cradling the little boys head.

My eyes got big, and I walked over and looked at the little boy, and I realized he did look just like Nike. Fuck! I didn't even say anything I ran out the door and headed towards my car. I had to get ghost because she was right Nike was gonna kill me when he found this out!

CHAPTER 9

*N*ike
I was sitting at my shop going over the numbers from both shop, things been looking up. I was thinking of starting a third shop. I was in a good place with my businesses, me and my son were building a relationship, and even me and Noni were getting along. She still wasn't trying to be with me, but I don't give a fuck she was still mine.

"Nigga hurry with that shit I'm trying to smoke and go to the strip club," Duke said busting through the door of my office.

"Man, I don't know why you still fuck with them damn things," I said laughing.

"Endless pussy." He said shrugging his shoulders.

Before I could respond my phone went off, I looked, and it was Noni calling.

"What up baby mama." I said soon as I answered.

"King you have to hurry and get to the hospital!" She yelled.

"Whoa, what's wrong."

"It's KJ some shit went down at my house, and he got pushed, and he hit his head, and he wouldn't wake up." By the point, I was pissed and was getting even more heated became she was hysterically crying.

"I'm on my way!" I said and hung up. I hopped up and ran towards the door. "Come on nigga we got to get to the hospital," I yelled running past Duke.

"What's wrong? He said.

"Something happen to KJ. Lock my door!" Nothing else was needed to be said. He locked the door and followed me to the front.

I rushed out and headed to my car and waited for Duke to get in before I started it and skirted off.

I cut a 25-minute ride into ten, I ran every light and stop sign. I swear if Noni told me some bullshit I might have to put my hands on her, and I'm not even that type of nigga.

I parked, and Duke and I rushed inside the emergency room doors. I went to the desk asking for my son and was directed where to go.

I saw Noni sitting down soon as I entered the room with her head in her hands. "What the fuck happened. I said. And where the fuck is my son!"

She whipped her head up and jumped up and ran over to me. She wrapped her around me and dug her face in my chest.

"Shonni what the fuck happened!" I wrapped my arms around her and looked down.

She looked up, and it was like something clicked. She stepped back and socked me in my mouth.

"Damn!" Duke yelled.

I grabbed my mouth, and my eyes popped open. I moved my hand from my lip and had fucking blood on my fingers.

"Yo, what the fuck!" I yelled.

"This is your fucking fault! She yelled.

"What are you talking about?" I walked over to the sink in the room and grabbed a few paper towels wiping my lip waiting for her to reply.

"Some bitch you're fucking came to my house thinking it was yours and attacked me and we fought, and she pushed my fucking son, and he hit his head on my table." She broke down crying again, and I stared at her confused, noticing the blood on her shirt before I walked over and grabbed her again.

"Shonni I need you to calm down and tell me what happened from beginning to end. I'm not even fucking anyone."

I looked at Duke, and he looked as lost as I was. After a few minutes, she finally calmed down enough talk and told me what happened. I asked her to explain what the girl looked like and as she began, I instantly knew who she was talking about.

"Was her name Evelynn?" I asked.

"You think that bitch did this? Duke said. I told you she was crazy man." I ignored him and kept my focused-on Noni.

"I don't know her name, but when I see her again, I'm beating her ass." She said.

"I'm going to take care of it, don't even worry about it. Where KJ?" I looked at Duke, and he was already on the phone putting things in motion.

She stared at me for a minute and then told me they took him to get a CT scan. "Aye BP about to come get me so we can get a handle on that. Duke said. Keep me updated." He walked over to Noni and kissed her forehead and dapped me up.

"Bet, soon as yall find that bitch hit my line," I said. He nodded and headed out the door.

Noni had gone and sat back down, and I walked over to the wall and leaned on it and stared at her.

"I'm sorry Noni, I haven't seen that bitch in over a month. I don't even know why she would pull this shit, she ain't even my bitch."

She didn't respond she looked up at me and then put her hands in her head. I pulled my phone out and tried to call Evelynn, but she didn't answer.

We sat there for a half an hour in silence both in our thoughts when the nurse finally brought KJ back in. He was sleeping on the bed, and she told us he had gotten ten staples in his head, but everything looked clear. Soon as she told me that I grew pissed all over again. I walked over to his bed and rubbed my hand over the top of his head.

"So, he's good to go home?" I asked.

"Yes, he's on pain medication right now, so he'll probably be sleep for the rest of the night. We're going to give you something to fight off a possible infection from the wound and also give him some medication to help with the headaches that may occur. Call his doctor in two weeks to remove the staples." The nurse said.

I didn't reply but Noni did ask a few more questions before the nurse left out. I hated seeing her so worried. After ten more minutes, the same nurse returned with discharge papers.

"Can you take us home please?" Noni asked as I picked up KJ. I started towards the door.

"How did you get here" I asked.

"I called an ambulance, I was scared to move KJ."

I nodded my head and glanced at my son.

"Nah, yall going back to my house." I said.

"No, were going home." I turned around and she had stopped and had her arms crossed over her chest.

I blew a deep breath out and walked towards her. "Look, I know your pissed at me and you haven't been trying to fuck with me since you been back, but right now you don't have a choice. I have one job right now and it's to keep both of yall safe and until Evelynn's dumb ass is taken care of then you'll be at my house."

I didn't even wait for her to answer or reply, I just turned around and continued towards the exit. I heard her mumbling, but I didn't care, this was on me, and until I fixed it, she would have to deal with it.

We got to my car and I put KJ in his booster seat and went and opened the door for Noni she got in and slammed the door. I chuckled a little to myself and walked over to my side.

I got in and started the car and headed towards my house. "Do you want to grab something to eat before we head home?" I asked and glanced at her.

"No, but I do need to run by my house and grab a few things if you're going to keep me hostage with you."

Instead of starting an argument, I changed the route and headed towards her house. A few minutes later I pulled in her driveway and parked and she hopped out. I waited in the car and texted Duke to see the update on Evelynn.

I looked up, and Noni was walking towards her car with a bag. I opened my door and got out the car.

"What are you doing man?" I asked.

"I'm going to follow you to your house, I have things to do and I'll need my car." She said.

"I have cars you can drive get in mine."

"I don't want to drive yours I want to drive mine, I just need to grab a few more things, and I'll be ready." I didn't answer instead I just watched her. After putting her bags in her car, she turned and headed back towards her house.

I ran my hand over my hair. I don't know how much more of her smart ass mouth I could take. I know all she needs is for me to put this dick in her to act right and she might just get that tonight if she kept this attitude up. I laughed and focused on her front door again once I heard it close.

"You ready now," I asked.

"Yeah, let's go."

She got in her car and started it, and I followed suit. I turned around and looked back at KJ, and he was still sleeping. I was so pissed I can't believe Evelynn's dumbass would do this and think it was ok. Soon as I got wind of her ass, I was killing her. I had told her to stay in her lane too many times and then brought Noni and my son into this, and he ended up in the hospital. That bitch better move to a whole different country because when I find her, it's over.

I pulled my phone out and made sure I kept my eyes on my review mirror to make sure Noni ass was still behind me. I tried to dial Evelynn again, but this time her phone was going straight to voice-mail. I know she was hiding, but as long as she was still in the city, we'd find her.

After 20 minutes, I pulled into my driveway with Noni right behind me. I got out and went to the back seat and open the door and grabbed KJ, who was finally coming to and waking up.

"Come on; I'll come back out and grab your bag after I open the door," I said.

This time she didn't argue she simply walked past me and headed toward the door. I followed behind her and opened the door when we got to it. I went straight to the stairs and walked up and headed to KJ's room so I could lay him down.

I laid him on his side, and he turned the opposite way, and I looked at the staples and felt my jaw clench together. I kissed his head and turned to walk out the door.

"Dad." I stopped and turned around.

"Yeah, son," I said.

"Can me and mommy stay here with you forever." He wasn't looking at me, and I was silent because I was taken back by that and didn't know what to say.

"We'll talk about it in the morning. Your head okay?"

"Yeah, I'm just sleepy."

"Go back to sleep; I'll have your mom come up and put your pajamas together."

"Okay, love you."

"Love you too son."

I walked out the room and leaned against the wall and ran my hand over my head and blew a breath out. I knew an argument was coming, but I didn't care my son wanted us together, and so did I. So Noni was gonna have to get with the program.

I pushed myself off the wall and headed towards my room to change and then went downstairs to the car to drag Noni and KJ's things out her car and prepared myself for this argument.

CHAPTER 10

*N*oni

Unknown: *Shonni quit playing with me and bring your ass home!*

Unknown: *I'm sorry for putting my hands on you, I changed and been taking classes it won't happen again.*

Unknown: *I know you ran back to your bitch ass baby daddy when that nigga fuck and leave you again don't come crying to me.*

Unknown: *Fuck that I'll be seeing you in a few days YOUR ASS IS MINE!*

I was sitting on the couch and when I read over the last message, and my heart dropped. Deshawn couldn't possibly know where I was. He knew where I was from but I never brought him home, so he was just talking out his ass, he had too.

As I was sitting there, my mind drifted off to when I first met Deshawn.

I was sitting at Starbucks working on a paper for school. KJ was only a couple months old, but I had found a really nice older lady to watch him for me while I was in school and when I needed to do school work. I was so focused on doing my paper I didn't even notice someone had sat down at my table until they tapped my hand.

I had pulled my hand back, and my head shot up. I hated being bothered when I was working on papers, but when I looked up, I couldn't complain.

Deshawn was so handsome. He was light skinned medium built with greenish brown eyes, he didn't have a lot of facial hair, but he did have a goatee. He had this baby face that made it look like he could do no harm. His hair was cut low, and he was sporting a Nike t-shirt and basketball shorts. He didn't have many tattoos, only to half sleeves on each side of his arms.

I stared at him, and he smiled showing his straight white teeth and the prettiest smile I had ever seen. I swear Deshawn should have been a male model because that was definitely the look he had.

"Don't you see I'm busy?" I asked rolling my eyes.

He chuckled and stared at me. "I'm sorry, but your beautiful and I would have felt right if I didn't come over and tell you that."

I blushed and tried not to smile. "You probably tell every girl you see that huh?"

"Nah, baby I only tell girls that when I mean it."

This time I laughed. "My name's Deshawn." He stuck his hand out for me to shake, but I just looked at it.

"I'm sorry I don't shake hands, people don't always wash them. But I'm Shonni."

From there I closed my laptop and found that Deshawn was someone who I could have a great conversation with. I learned he was a fire fighter and three years older than me. I told him about KJ from the jump and explained that I didn't deal with his father. We clicked instantly, and he asked me out on a date after I agreed he left and I couldn't even focus on my paper anymore.

We went on a couple of dates before I introduced him to KJ and we made it official. After a year of dating, we moved in with each other, and I was completely in love that I ignored the signs. Deshawn would raise his voice and get mad over little things. He would mug me and push me when we would argue and then eventually a pushed turned into a slap and only escalated from there.

I was so dead set on finishing school to provide for my son in the future that I stayed and took the abuse. I had nowhere to go, I could have moved out and continued to struggle like I was before Deshawn but I wanted better for my son and Deshawn wasn't letting me go.

I didn't have any friends down there and from what he told me his parents were dead and he didn't have any siblings so there was no one I could turn to for help.

The day he thought it was okay to put his hands on my son, however, was the day I had to leave. I didn't care what he did to me but my son was a child, and not even his child and I refused to let Deshawn abuse him.

I started saving money away and secretly moving my things out the house little by little. I had stopped having sex with him and was sleeping on the couch or in the bed with KJ. I had talked my mom into getting an apartment in her name for me so that he couldn't find me and two months later I left and never seen Deshawn again. I got all my classes switched to video chat, and I changed my number. Once graduated I packed me and my son up and headed back to Miami.

I heard the door slam shut, knocking me out my day dream. It scared me so bad I nearly had a heart attack. I jumped so hard I felt myself get whip lash.

"What the fuck you jumping for?" King asked sitting my bags down.

I went to respond, and my words got caught in my throat. King was shirtless and just in basketball shorts and socks. My eyes traveled down between his legs and my mouth watered.

I haven't been with King since my graduation night when I got pregnant with KJ. I missed having sex with him even though we only did it twice both times were forever embedded in my memory. Having sex with Deshawn these couple's years didn't even compare to having sex with King and I barely even had an orgasm with Deshawn unless he was giving me head.

I heard King clear his throat and I felt my cheeks get red. "Unless you want him all up in yo shit and possibly get yo ass pregnant again I advise you not to be staring.

I smacked my lips and rolled my eyes. "No one is worried about yo ugly ass!"

He laughed. "Yeah okay, just don't be staring at a nigga like that anymore then." My phone went off again, and I was pretty sure it was Deshawn. I don't even know how he got my new number.

"Who the fuck is texting you this late?" I looked down at my phone, and it was only going on ten o clock.

"King, it's only ten o clock chill. Plus, it might be my nigga." I rolled my eyes and looked at him, and he had a mug on his face.

"Yeah okay, let that be yo nigga and see how long yall last when I find out who he is."

"You're not my man, so you have no right to threaten anyone I deal with."

"Yeah okay tell yoself that Shonni but once you pushed my son out of that pretty ass pussy of yours, I got every right in the world. Matter fact the first time I stuck my dick in you and popped yo cherry I had every right. Which reminds me, you were fucking that fuck nigga you were with?"

I was caught off guard and wasn't expecting the conversation to go that way. I felt my face ball up, it wasn't any of his business, but I knew he wasn't going to let it go if I didn't answer him.

"He was my boyfriend King, of course, I had sex with him."

I hesitantly looked up at him, and he was clenching his jaw and staring dead at me. I got nervous and began playing with my fingers but surprisingly he didn't say anything he just turned, and head for the stairs and I knew he was pissed but what did he think, I was gonna be Virgin Mary until he got his shit together. I shrugged and walked over to our bags and followed him and searched the rooms upstairs until I found the one my son was in.

I walked in, sat the bags down, and over to the bed and sat down. I rubbed his back and kissed his head. I couldn't believe that that crazy bitch had the nerve to push my baby. I thank God, he was okay though. I decided he could bathe in the morning he had, had a long night so I changed him into his pajamas and took his shoes off and kissed him one last time.

I followed the weed smell and found King's room. I knocked, but he didn't answer the door. I opened the door anyway and he was laying down in his bed smoking a blunt and in his phone, was in his other hand.

"Which room am I staying in?" I asked.

"There's empty rooms ain't it? Pick one." He said coldly.

I rolled my eyes. "You ain't have to say it like I was bothering you."

"You are bothering me."

I was kind of taken back, but I knew he was in his feelings because the thought of my fucking Deshawn was in his head.

"Well, I didn't ask to be here you made me!" I said crossing my arms over my chest.

"If you want to leave, then get the fuck out but don't take my fucking son out of here. I'm not playing."

"Who the fuck are you talking to?" My hands were now on my hips, and my eyes had tears threatening to fall.

"I'm not about to keep kissing your ass and dealing with yo smart ass mouth Shonni. I've killed mutha fucka for less. So, like I said if you don't want anything else get the fuck out and leave me alone."

I didn't say anything else instead I turned and made sure I slammed his door behind me. Fuck him. I know I had been a bitch to him lately, but did he really blame me. I went and grabbed my bag out of KJ's room and went to the room next door and went and sat on the bed.

I would stay here tonight because I wasn't leaving my son, but first thing in the morning when he woke up we were leaving. I wiped my eyes and decided to take a shower. I was dead tired and crying over Kingston was something I promised myself I would never do again.

I was having a wet dream about King and didn't want to open my eyes because I didn't want it to stop. He was in between my legs sucking the soul out of me. I let out a soft moan and arched my back a little.

"Fuck King." I let escape my lips.

I moved my hands down between my legs, and my legs shot open when I felt a head full of hair.

"King? What are you-FUCK!" I yelled out.

He looked up at me and stuck his finger in me and began to suck on my clit. I tried to move up, and he took his finger out me and gripped my legs and began tongue fucking my pussy. Feeling his thick, long tongue go across my clit caused me to look at him. Soon as I made eye contact with him again, I was cumming.

He continued to suck on my clit like he was trying to get every drop. He stuck his finger in me again and motioned it forward as if he was saying come here and began spelling his name with his tongue and I came again and harder this time.

I was drained, but I wanted some dick after that. I knew I was hurt by how King acted early, but I know some of that anger was on me and what happened to our son. It had been so long since King had been inside me, that I was literally about to cry waiting for him to enter me, but to my surprise, he didn't. In fact, he looked at me with a smirk and wiped his mouth with the back of his and hand and got off the bed and headed out the door.

"Wait, what are you doing?" I leaned up and stared at him. He didn't say anything though he kept walking and shut the door behind him. I was so confused on what just happen, and even though I wanted to fuck Kingston, I was just happy he made me cum back to back. I got comfortable again and went to sleep with my mind at peace.

CHAPTER 11

Deshawn

I just got off the plane, and I was already ready to go back to Atlanta. The Miami heat hit me instantly, and I became even more pissed off that I'm even here chasing after Shonni's ungrateful ass. After everything I did for the bitch she just up and left me. Even after helping her take care of her bastard ass son. I know when I do catch up to her she's leaving that little nigga here, we'll make some more with my blood running through them.

I was meeting up with my cousin because she said she knew where Shonni and her bitch ass baby daddy were and if that nigga had a problem with me getting my girl and taking her home, then I'll just have to kill him.

After I got my rental and everything I went to my hotel to drop my things off then texted my cousin asking her where and when she wanted to meet up. Once she gave me the location, I grabbed what I needed and headed out.

I pulled in the restaurant and soon as I walked in eyes were on me. I was a sexy nigga, and maybe one of these bitches might get blessed with the dick tonight, but right now only one thing was on my mind. I saw my cousin ducked off in the corner.

"It's about time you showed up!" She said looking around.

"Don't start with the attitude Eve; I'm not in the mood. I said. Why the fuck are you in the corner looking like the police is after you anyway."

"I fucked up Shawn, really bad."

I squinted my eyes and looked at her for a minute; she didn't look like she was on drugs, so that was out.

"What the fuck you do?"

She took and deep breath and explained her situation to me. "So, you know where her house is?"

"Shawn, is that seriously all you're worried about? Kingston is going to kill me!"

"Fuck Kingston and his son. I'm here to bring my girl home and if them niggas get in the way they got to go." She looked at me with her mouth wide open.

"You'll kill an innocent child?"

"He's a fucking spoiled brat who Shonni babied too much. All his ass did was cry and complain. And shit he ain't my son so why do I give a fuck."

She shook her head. "I always told Aunt Maggy something was wrong with you."

"Look do you want me to help you with this problem or not?"

"Yes, but I don't want Kingston to die! I love him, I just need Shonni out the way and then I can apologize for his son and explain what happened, and we can be together."

This time I looked at her like she was crazy. "Come on if you're that scared of this nigga you can't, believe he's gonna just be okay with you pushing his son and just forgive you."

"He will once I explain to him what happened. That dumb bitch probably told him a lie anyway."

"Look, I got some shit I need to do, so send me her address and I'll handle the rest."

I didn't even wait for her to answer. I stood up and turned and walked towards the door before I stopped and turned around and looked at her.

"Stay out the way for a while, shoot me where you're staying too. But I need you off the radar for a while. I got this."

With that, I turned and continued out the door. Evelyn better take heed to my warning and stay out the way, or I would have to get rid of her too.

After I left the restaurant, I drove to my next destination. I got out the car and was impressed this nigga was doing his thing. If I didn't want to kill the nigga I might have actually had him hook me up.

I walked in and looked around, the place was even nicer on the inside.

"Welcome to Deluxe Wheels, can I help you?" I turned towards the voice and seen a young pretty light skinned girl behind a desk.

"Yeah, I'm looking for the owner," I said looking around.

"He actually is busy at the moment. Did you have a complaint?"

"Nah, I'm looking to get my car done, but I want to talk to the man himself."

"Well I can set you up with an appointment, and you can meet with him on a different day."

I thought for a minute. That could work I had to go scoop out Shonni's house anyway.

"Cool set me up with something, the soonest he's available."

Once I was squared away with part one of my plan, I decided to go get some food and head back to the room. Tomorrow I was gonna go see what was going on over Shonni's I would give it a few days but her ass had me fucked up if she thought she wasn't leaving with me.

CHAPTER 12

*T*rina

    I was sitting at my vanity doing my make up getting ready for my date. I hadn't seen Duke since I snuck in his house a few weeks ago and since then he's been avoiding me like I had the plague. I wasn't used to the feelings I was having for him. I had always seen Duke as my brother, so I wasn't sure how to handle this.

Tonight, though I was pushing those thoughts to the side and was going out with this dude Lawrence, he had been trying to talk to me for a while. He worked at my brother's shop, and he was cute, so I decided to give him a chance.

I had on a black v cut shirt, and a pair of dark Levi's I was keeping it simple instead of rocking all designer. I had on a pair of all black retro 12's.

I decided to meet him at the restaurant because if I wasn't feeling him best believe I was leaving his ass right at the restaurant. Hopefully, we made it past dinner because a bitch ain't had no dick in a while and I needed a release.

I checked myself out one last time and headed out the door. It took me 10 minutes to get the restaurant and find a parking spot.

I walked in and was greeted by the hostess immediately.

"How many?" She said.

"I'm actually meeting someone," I said.

"What's the name?"

"Jamison"

"Yes, he's here."

I followed behind her and was impressed by the place Lawrence had chosen.

I sat down and smiled once we reached the table.

"I'm happy you finally decided to give a nigga a chance." He said licking his lips and lustfully staring at me.

I looked him over and admired his peanut butter skin and full lips. His brown eyes complimented his skin color, and his low-cut hair fit his face.

"I know what did I have to lose."

"Ouch, he laughed, was that a compliment." I didn't say anything instead I shrugged.

"So, Trina why are you single?"

"Because I like to be able to fuck whoever I want when I want and not answer to anyone."

He laughed. "Well, at least you're honest."

"Of course, most guys aren't faithful and growing up with my brother showed me how much of dog these niggas could be, so I decided not to let myself get played like the rest of these dumb bitches.

He nodded and smirked. "I respect that. A lot of females wouldn't be honest but you ain't sugar coat shit. So, you wouldn't consider being in a relationship?"

"I mean if I met a guy who showed he was worth me changing then of course. But I'm not about to be with a nigga and he dogging me out, fucking other bitches."

"I agree, but it ain't all us niggas. You females be on that shit too."

I shrugged my shoulders "Shit you right; I guess we ain't shit either." We looked at each other, and both laughed.

The rest of dinner was nothing but good vibes and conversation. I enjoyed spending this time with him, so much that I was now following him back to his house to get my back blown out.

I pulled in after him and got out and followed him up to his apartment. I waited for him to open the door and soon as he did he turned and picked me up and tried to kiss me but I wasn't feeling that so I turned my head and he went to my neck instead. I wrapped my legs around him and he turned and kicked his door shut and headed down the hall to what I assumed was his bed room.

I was horny as hell and didn't want foreplay, so I hope he didn't try it. "You're sexy as fuck Trina. He said against my neck. Fuck I can't wait to feel you."

He gently threw me on the bed and then pulled me down to the edge by my ankles. "It's been a while; can we please just skip all this." He nodded, and I pulled my shirt off and threw it on the floor and grabbed my pants and began pulling them off before taking over. He pulled my shoes off first then he yanked my pants down and began to kiss the inside of my thighs.

I guess I could get some head before I get some dick. He began kissing the outside of my lips threw my panties, and I threw my head back. I just need an orgasm. I didn't know what was wrong with me. I was never this horny before I had sex with Duke and he blew my back out. Fuck there I go thinking about his sexy ass again.

"Trina!" I snapped out of it and looked down.

"Yeah?" I said.

"You cool, you don't seem into this."

I nodded. "Yeah, I'm sorry, I told you I didn't want foreplay."

He didn't say anything instead he stood up and took his pants off. He walked over to his dresser and grabbed a condom from in it and pulled his boxers off.

His dick was average size, he definitely wasn't bigger than Dukes. I shook my head; Duke wasn't my nigga I had to get him out my head.

He began stroking himself before he ripped the condom open and put it on. I leaned back on my elbows, and he walked over the bed and leaned over me and pulled my panties off. He placed his dick at the tip of my opening and push in.

I swear I wanted to laugh when the nigga started stroking. He was like a dog in heat humping me like a jack rabbit. What's worse is he was talking shit.

Now I wasn't the type to fake if I wasn't feeling it, but I refused to leave here without cumming.

"Lawrence wait." I pushed my hand against his chest.

"What's wrong? I'm not hurting you, am I?" I looked at him like he was crazy. If he meant humping me like he was a 13-year-old virgin losing his virginity for the first time then yes.

"No, I just want to get on top." He smiled and got from off me, and I moved and let him lay down. I looked and made sure the condom was still intact and climbed on him. Once I was on him, I begin moving up and down finding my rhythm and rocking my hips. I began clenching my pussy muscles together and rocking faster. I was determined to cum.

Not even five minutes of me being on top this nigga came I stopped and looked down. "Are you fucking serious right now?" I yelled hopping off him.

"Fuck man, yo pussy was too good. I couldn't hold that shit in." I was so disgusted and disappointed. I didn't even say anything, I began to pick my clothes and putting them on. I was so pissed at this nigga I couldn't even look at him. He didn't seem bothered, in fact, he was sitting on his bed rolling a blunt, I didn't even know where he got it from. I grabbed my shoes not even bothering to put them on and walked towards the door. I made sure I slammed it on my way out too.

I got in my car and threw my shoes in my passenger seat and started my car and headed home to my vibrator that would surely get the job done.

The next morning, I woke up I decided to text Noni and see if she wanted to meet up and get our nails and stuff done. Nike told me what that bitch Evelynn did to my nephew, and that bitch better hope I don't see her because I was fucking her up on sight.

Shonni agreed to meet up; she was taking KJ to my mom's in an hour, so I had time to waste until then. I went to the bathroom and showered and handled my hygiene. Soon as I finished drying off, I had the urge to throw up. I ran back into the bathroom and hurled in the toilet. I began to dry heave barely having anything in my stomach to throw up.

After I rinsed my mouth out and brushed my teeth again and I went back into my room and got dressed. I threw on a simple maxi dress with a thong that made my ass have a little more bounce to it.

I went in my kitchen and made me some cereal, but soon as I tasted the milk, I was over the garbage can throwing up again. I swear that restaurant gave me food poisoning. After I went and brushed my teeth again, I decided to just head to my mom's house and meet Noni there.

When I got to my mom's, I had to clench my thighs together because I saw Duke's car outside. Like I said it had been a couple of weeks since I last seen him and after last night I could just hop right on him in front of everyone.

I parked and headed inside, and Nike and Duke were sitting on the couch.

"Hey yall, I said, Noni here?"

"Why would she be here?" He asked not looking at me.

"Because she's dropping my grandson off." My mom said coming out the dining room.

I walked over to the couch and tapped Duke on the head.

"You can't speak ugly boy." He turned and looked at me and licked his lips and my pussy jumped. I bit my lip and stared at his mouth.

"What's up Tri?" He said.

I frowned. "I hate when you call me that."

"That's why I do it." He said laughing.

I rolled my eyes and turned and looked at my mom who was staring at me. "Why are yo looking at me like that?"

"You got something to tell us?" My heart began beating in my stomach. Was she talking about Duke. I looked over at Duke and both him and Nike were staring at me.

Thank God when I was about to answer KJ came busting through the door with Noni right after him.

"Hey yall." She said.

No one answered though my mom was still staring at me but hugging KJ who come right in and hugged her.

"I made you some food KJ go in the dining room and eat baby."

"Okay Grammy!" He said and took off towards the dining room.

"What's going on?" Noni said looking at each of us.

"Trina was just about to announce she's pregnant." I swear the I started choking on air, me and Duke both.

"Mom what are you talking about?" I screeched.

"Yo heard me, I thought so couple weeks ago because of how your boobs grew and you got a little thicker. But now looking at you I'm for sure now."

"Come on mom if Trina was pregnant she would tell us."

"Kingston I've had two kids I know what pregnancy looks like, her hips have spread, she gets irritated faster, and her nose is a little fatter too. You been throwing up?"

This time I looked at Duke and his eyes were glued to me not saying anything but hanging on to every word.

"I mean I did this morning but I think the food I ate on my date made me sick."

"Date!" I looked over and Duke now had his face balled up. I wasn't entertaining him though. I thought about what my mom said and what if I was pregnant. I'd be pregnant with Dukes baby, shit!

CHAPTER 13

𝒩oni

I looked over at Trina, and she looked like she was about to shit bricks. I looked her over, and her mom was right she had gained weight and seeing her in that dress you could see a small pudge in her midsection.

Trina didn't tell me she was seeing anyone so if she was pregnant who the hell was the dad. I remember her telling me about her date, but this was the first time she decided to go out with the guy so who the hell had she be fucking.

I knew she wasn't gonna say anything right here and especially in front of her brother. Speaking of him we literally have become room-mates it had been a week since he snuck in my room and ate the soul out of me and we've barely spoken since then.

We make small conversation when KJ's around, but that's it. I knew he was fed up with my attitude and KJ wanted us to be one happy family, but I couldn't just forget about the past. I wanted to be with him, I still loved him and being around his every day was torture. Like right now looking at him mugging the hell out of Trina was sexy as hell.

I wonder if he was fucking bitches. I hear him walk around whispering on the phone and he was out late a lot. I didn't know what he did in the streets outside his shops I knew he had an alternate income at one point, but I wasn't sure if he was still had it. But I know that wasn't what was keeping him out late. I knew that it wasn't my place to be mad, but I was. I shook my head and turned my attention back to Trina who still hadn't spoken.

"Mom, you're crazy I just been eating good, I'm not pregnant. I'm on birth control anyway." She finally said.

I looked at her and noticed how she kept looking at Duke, and his ass was staring a hole in her. Hell, no I know she wasn't fucking Duke.

"Trina go buy a test and take it because I promise you're pregnant."

"Who the fuck are you fucking Trina!" King yelled. He stood up crossing his muscular arms across his chest.

"Nike I'm grown, who I have sex with is none of your business."

"Bet, when I find out who it is I'm beating that nigga's ass. Let's go, Duke." He didn't wait for anyone to respond he headed towards the door and stopped in front of me and looked me up and down.

"Who the fuck told you to come out the house wearing that?" I bit my lip, I loved when he tried to boss up on me, and that sexy ass mug was back on his face.

"Nike watch your damn mouth!" His mom yelled.

I looked down at my outfit and back up at him. I had on a sun dress; I didn't see the problem.

"I have a dress on King, what's the issue?"

"Why is it so short? You gone make me fuck you up too." His phone went off, and he looked at it and ignored whoever it was.

"Who is that?" I asked putting my hands on my hips.

"A bitch I'm fucking who wants me to slide through." He said shrugging his shoulders.

"Kingston!" His mom yelled.

"I hate you," I said looking him dead in his eyes.

He chuckled and leaned down close to my ear and whispered. "If you would stop playing I'd cut all these hoes off." He turned and faced me and pecked my lips, pulled back and winked at me. I tried to fight the smile off my lips, even after the bullshit he said. He

4 EVER DOWN WITH HIM

turned and continued towards the door with Duke following behind.

'Let's go too Noni.' Trina said following behind the boys.

"Don't yo fast ass forget to go buy a test!" Momma T yelled after her. She stopped and frowned at her mom but didn't say anything just kept towards the door.

I laughed and turned and faced her. "KJ come here," I yelled. I waited a few seconds, and he came running out.

"I'm leaving be good for Grammy." He nodded, and I bent down and kissed his cheek. "I'll see you guys later."

I walked out the door, and Trina and King were outside arguing, and Duke sat there with a mug on his face.

"Nike I'm not pregnant leave it alone!" She yelled grabbing her door handle.

"Yeah alright, momma right you have gained weight."

"Good dick will do that to you." I laughed, and she shrugged her shoulders.

"I'm going to fuck you up! Go buy a test. He looked at me. Make sure she buys one." I rolled my eyes and headed to her passenger door and got in.

She didn't say anything back to him either she just got in and started her car and reversed out and headed towards the nail shop.

"Bitch spill the tea, you fucking Duke?" I asked after a long silence between us. We had about ten more minutes till we got to the nail salon, so she was gonna talk.

"Why the fuck would you ask me that. You know Duke is like my brother." She glanced at me quickly and hurried and turned her focus back to the road.

"Bitch don't think I didn't notice the glances yall kept throwing at each other and how he almost choked to death when yo mom asked if you were pregnant."

She didn't say anything instead she busted out crying. "It wasn't supposed to happen! I swear we were drunk the night of his party and I don't know it just happened.

"Trina calm down before you crash! It's not that big of a deal."

She started to control her breathing and stopped crying so hard.

"You know my brother he's gonna be pissed when he finds out. I don't want to come between them. But what if I am pregnant what am I gonna do, me and Duke aren't together we grew up together and we're both hoes."

I tried not to laugh, but I couldn't help it. Trina was so dramatic, but she always kept it real.

"Trina chill, if you're pregnant then you are you know Duke will be there for you."

"He won't have that choice because I'm not about to keep it."

I looked at her like she was crazy. "Trust me abortion isn't the solution. I felt like shit after mine, and I regret it even to this day.

"What am I going to do with a baby though. I should have never taken it there with Duke."

"Well you did, and it's a possibility you might be having his baby. He is the only possible guy, right?"

"Yes, bitch! Hoe might be life is what I live by, but I always make sure they wrap up. My dumbass just didn't think to make Duke besides I'm on birth control.

"Look let's go get our nails and feet done and after we'll grab a test and figure things out from there." She didn't say anything instead she nodded her head and wiped her eyes.

"Everything's going to be okay Trina, don't stress yourself out about it."

We continued to the nail shop, and I sent a text to Lo telling her to meet us, Jay was with his dad, so I knew she was free. I had never seen Trina so upset, and that was another indicator she could be pregnant. I wouldn't tell her, but I was excited thinking about her being pregnant with my God kid.

We got to the nail salon, and Lo was sitting in her car waiting on us. I told Trina to park next to her, and we got out the car and Lo came over and hugged both of us.

"What's wrong with her?" She asked.

"She's pregnant," I said nonchalantly.

"Bitch!" Trina said cutting her eyes at me.

I shrugged my shoulders.

"Bitch congrats."

Trina ignored her and started towards the nail salon. I laughed, and me and Lo followed behind her.

❧

*W*e were sitting in front of the bathroom, and Trina had just taken the test, and we were waiting for the results.

"So, you might be having Duke's baby. Bitch at least yo baby gone look good, Duke sexy ass fuck." Lo boasted. Trina cut her eyes at her.

"Bitch don't play with me."

Lo laughed. "Chill sis, you know I wouldn't do that." I laughed too because Trina was seriously emotional as fuck now.

The timer went off, and we looked at Trina who didn't budge. I got up and walked into the bathroom and grabbed some toilet paper and wrapped it around the test and walked out without looking at it.

"What does it say? She said.

I looked down and began to smile. "Bitch, you're about to be a mom!"

Trina rushed over and snatched the test out my hands and shook her head. "I'm about to be a mom. I'm having a baby, by Duke." She said quietly.

I felt for my girl because Nike was going to be pissed and I wasn't sure how Duke would take it either, but I was going to be there for her every step of the way supporting her.

CHAPTER 14

*E*velynn

I was so tired of hiding out. I heard Nike was looking for me and I knew it was gonna take a lot of begging for me to forgive him.

How the fuck was I supposed to know that bitches' son was his or that he was gonna come and try to grab me. When the fuck did he get a kid anyway. I wasn't sure if I was ready to be a step mom but to be with Nike, I was willing to make that sacrifice

I took a deep breath and decided to call Nike and see if we could meet up. I clicked his name and waited for him to answer.

"Hello," I said looking and seeing he had answered.

"What's up?" He said.

"Nike look I know you're looking for me, but I want to apologize for pushing your son."

"Oh yeah?"

"Yeah, I didn't know it was your son, and the stupid bitch attacked me."

"You ran up in the house, what the fuck was she supposed to do?"

"I was looking for you!"

"You're not my bitch Evelynn I don't know why it's so hard for you to understand."

Knock. Knock. Knock.

"Nike, I gotta go!"

"Wait I miss hitting that shit. Can we meet up."

I bit my lip remembering the long strokes he used to give me.

"You swear you're not mad anymore."

"I just fucking told you I wasn't if you don't want meet then fuck it."

"NO! Okay, let's meet this weekend."

"Bet I'll call you." With that, I hung in smiling. I knew he was going to forgive me. His stupid ass baby mom was irrelevant at this point.

I forgot someone was at my door till the pounding started again.

I walked over to it and made sure I looked first and opened the door.

"Why the fuck it take you so long to answer the door?" Shawn yelled pushing past me.

I was already ready for him to go back to Atlanta. I forgot this nigga was bat shit crazy.

"Look I just talked to Nike so- "

He grabbed me by my neck. "Bitch why the fuck are you talking to him. I told you to stay out the way."

I started scratching at his hands trying to get him off.

He began to laugh and let me go shoving me to the ground.

"What the fuck!" I yelled struggling to breathe.

"Stay the fuck away from him, and if I feel like you on some funny shit I'll kill yo ass too!" With that, he turned and walked back out the door.

I didn't know what to do about him but I knew for sure I had to warn Nike and stay the fuck out of Shawn's way.

CHAPTER 15

*N*ike

"So, am I going to see you tonight?" I clenched my jaw to stop myself from cussing this bitch out.

"Taliyah, I already told you I had shit to do man."

"But Nike I miss you, it been two days." She whined.

Taliyah was this bad little light skin chick I had met one day I was at the mall buying me and KJ these J's that had just released. We had been seeing each other a little over a month now, and she was clingy as fuck.

I hadn't fucked her yet because she was spitting some get to know each other shit but her head was fire, so I was cool, I had other bitches I could call up for some pussy.

The other day when I was at my mom's house Taliyah was blowing my shit up I know Noni was mad, but I was telling the truth soon as she said the word everyone was gone.

"Nike are you listening to me!"

"What man?"

"Can you come over after I get off?" She was a nurse at a nursing home and usually worked till late at night.

"Only way I'm getting out my bed in the middle of the night I if I'm getting some pussy."

"What if I'm ready for it tonight."

"Oh, word?"

"Nike, I need to talk to you!" Noni said busting through my door.

"Who the fuck is that?" Taliyah yelled.

"Aye call me when you get off," I said and hung up.

"Yo ass can't knock," I said fucking with her.

"Who were you talking to on the phone?" She asked.

"Why you in my business?"

"Because you didn't have to rush off the phone because I came in."

"I know I didn't, but I figured since you busted in here you needed something."

"When am I going home?" I looked up at her and admired her thick ass thighs in the little ass shorts she was always wearing around the house.

"We're a family Noni why you trying to leave?"

"Because we are not together King, I have a life and being here with you is messing everything up."

"What the fuck is it messing up?"

She didn't say anything at first instead she played with her hands and avoided eye contact with me.

"I want to start dating again King."

I glared at her. "What the fuck do you mean you want to start dating again."

"Just what I said. I'm not getting any younger."

"So, what you want to find another fuck nigga huh?"

She rolled her eyes and placed her hands on her thick ass hips. "No Nike I want to find someone who loves me and wants to build with me. I start school next month and I'm at a point in my life where I'm ready to find someone to share this moment with me, eventually have more kids."

"So, what the fuck am I? I'm trying to give you that!"

"By fucking all these different bitches? By being out all night and keeping me here hostage because you couldn't keep your bitches in check?"

"Why does it matter who I'm sticking my dick in, you ain't letting me stick it in you." I shrugged my shoulders.

"You know what, fuck you I'm taking my fucking son and I'm going back home. It was a mistake to ever bring you back in my life."

I hopped off the bed and rushed her making her back into the wall.

"What the fuck did you just say?"

She swallowed hard, and I saw the tears form in her eyes. "Why the fuck you crying, say what you just said again," I yelled, and she flinched. I was so pissed I forgot her bitch ass ex used to beat her ass.

I punched the wall, and she lost it and broke down crying and slid down pulling her legs into her in holding them.

"I'm sorry King." She cried.

"Fuck man, Shonni get up I'm sorry baby."

I reached down to grab her, and she jumped and tried to scoot back. I swear I needed to get on finding her bitch ass ex this shit was breaking my heart. She was terrified, and all I did was raise my voice.

I bent down and picked her up and carried her to my bed. I laid her down, and she balled up and kept crying. I sat down and pulled her into me.

"He used to get mad at the littlest things, and at first it started off as little arguments and him raising his voice." She whispered. I didn't say anything; she needed this.

"Then he would push me and call me stupid or something that made me feel less than him. Then one day one of my classmates offered to take me home because my battery had died and Deshawn wouldn't answer, so I agreed to let him. We pulled at the same time as Deshawn, and he gave me the deadliest stare. I thanked the guy from school and hurried and the house, and soon as he got in the house, he slapped the shit out me.

She stopped talking for a minute. I can tell she trying to get herself together.

Then he grabbed me by my hair and asked if I was cheating on him and I tried to explain what happened, and he told me I should have called an Uber a threw me to the ground."

"Why didn't you leave him." I had to make my voice sound as calm as possible because I wanted to break some shit.

"I wanted to. I even tried, but I was a single parent and a college student. Before I got with Deshawn, I was struggling, and I didn't want to go through that again. I left and went to a hotel for a few days with KJ, and he begged me to come back and apologized. When I went back home, he beat my ass for leaving and thought I was laid up with some nigga.

The night I caught him cheating on me I told him I was done and I was leaving and he like blacked out and began fighting me like a nigga. He was choking me, and KJ ran in the room trying to grab me, and he pushed him into the wall and knocked the wind out my baby." She stopped talking and looked at me.

"King I swear after that I was officially done. I know I should have been left but I didn't, but after he did that to KJ I left. When I finally left KJ finally told me he hated Deshawn because he always yelled at him and made me cry and would threaten to beat him if he told me how he felt. I didn't know I swear I didn't!" She started crying hard all over again, and I grabbed her into my arm and let her cry on my chest.

"Noni stop crying man. I got you and KJ; I swear to you I'm going to take care of that nigga. He's dead and that's on my son. I wish you would have reached out to me and told me what was going on and you guys wouldn't have gone through that."

"I've been so bitter because of the shit I went through in high school that I let it get in the way of your relationship with KJ. I let my son be scared half his life because I was in my feelings."

"I'm here now, and you don't have to worry about that bitch ass nigga okay." She nodded and snuggled close to me.

"Can I sleep in here tonight," I told her yes with no hesitation, and for the first time since she's been at my house, I just wanted to hug her and nothing more.

I got to the shop around 11 the next day I had some meeting with some nigga who only wanted to deal with the boss, so here I was.

I walked in, and Janet shifted her head to the side when I made eye contact with her. I followed her eyes and seen some nigga sitting down on his phone. I walked over and stood in front of him.

85

"You the dude who thought my staff wasn't good enough for you?" I asked.

He looked up at me with a smirk and put his phone away. "Nah, nothing like that." He stood up and reached his hand out, and I grabbed it and shook it.

"Andre." He said.

"Follow me in my office, Andre."

I told him to sit down and closed the door behind us. I walked behind my desk and stared at him. It was something about this nigga I didn't trust, but I couldn't tell what it was just yet.

"What can I do for you, Andre?" I asked looking him in the eyes.

"I just moved here, and I'm big on cars, and I want mine personalized, but I want some shit not everyone has and I did some research, and your place is a big deal."

"So why do you want to deal with just me, my crew is more than capable getting your car how you want."

"I'm sure they are, but I wanted to see the face behind the business before I made my final decision."

I chuckled a little. "Look I don't know what your angle is, but I'm not for the games so tell me why you really wanted to meet with me."

He didn't answer her looked the picture on my desk and grabbed it. "This your girl?" It was a picture of Shonni and KJ I had developed.

"Why the fuck is that any of your business." Now I was getting pissed.

He placed the picture down and threw is hands up. "No disrespect just was going to say you're lucky she's a beauty." I mugged him and stood up and walked to my door and opened it.

"If you want to do business make an appointment to bring your car in with Janet if not get the fuck out." He smirked at me and nodded and got up to walk towards the door.

"Nice talking to you Kingston, I'll be seeing."

"Mutha fucka the fuck you just say." He didn't say anything though he just walked out and towards the main door. I didn't know who that nigga was, but I was gonna find out and soon.

CHAPTER 16

*D*uke

I was currently at the mall with this little jump off I chilled with from time to time. Farrah was someone I had been messing with for about six months now. She was a part of the National Guard, so she wasn't always here, but whenever she came home, we met up.

We were currently in line at the food court grabbing something to eat. She had me hold her damn bags like I was her personal butler or some shit but it was cool. Farrah wasn't extra, she knew her spot in my life, and she never over stepped that. We texted from time to time, and we fucked, went out to eat, and shopped at times when she came to town but it was nothing but a friendship with her, and we both were okay with that.

"Can we grab something to drink I'm thirsty," I swear my head whipped in the direction of the voice I had just heard so quick.

"Hold up Farrah I'll be right back," I said.

I handed her, her bags and walked over to Trina. "What's up Tri, who's this?" I said startling her and causing her to turn around and stare at me.

She sat there stuck on stupid and cleared her throat. "What are you doing here?" She said trying to put some base in her voice.

I chuckled and turned and looked at dude. "Why I'm here doesn't matter. Who's your friend?"

She blew a breath out, and I smirked at her. "This is Ashur." She rolled her eyes, and I eyed her admiring the little ass shorts and tank top she had on until I got to her stomach and remembered what her mom said. I heard my name being called, but I never took my eyes off her stomach.

When she noticed me looking at it, she quickly pulled her bags in front of it. I darted my eyes up to hers, but she refused to meet them.

"Trina who is this?" Dude asked.

"I'm sorry Ashur, this is my brother's friend Duke." She said. I laughed as she tried to downplay me.

"Duke you didn't hear me calling you," Farrah asked walking up to us.

Fuck I forgot I was here with her. "My bad, I just saw Nike's sister and decided to speak." I said grabbing her bags from her but not taking my eyes off Trina if she wanted to play then so be it.

"I didn't know Nike had a sister. I'm Farrah." She said reaching her hand out, but Trina petty ass turned her nose up.

"Let's go Ashur." She turned and started walking away and didn't wait for him to answer.

"What's her deal?" She asked looking at me. I shrugged but didn't answer. Trina had me so fucked up right now, and Farrah was the least of my worries.

I took my phone out and sent Trina a text telling her she had 20 minutes to get rid of dude and meet me at my crib or I was showing my ass and didn't give a fuck who seen me.

I told Farrah I had some shit to handle, but I would see her before she headed back out. I was happy we drove separate because her ass was going to be shit out of luck getting home. I stopped by the drug store before I headed home.

I pulled up and seen Trina's car sitting outside. I got out, grabbed my bag, and walked over to it, and it was empty.

When I got in the house, Trina was sitting on my couch stuffing her face. I smiled and walked over to her sat the bag on the floor, and sat down next to her. I grabbed a piece of chicken and started eating. She looked at me with an evil glare and continued eating.

I let her finish eating and then she turned and looked at me. "Why did you call me here? I know it wasn't just to watch me eat." I picked the bag up off the floor and reached in and handed her the box.

She screwed her face up and looked her me. "Why are you giving me a pregnancy test?" I didn't answer right away. Instead I poked at her stomach.

"You never had a gut before."

"Are you calling me fat?"

"Quick fucking playing with me Trina." I stood up and grabbed her and pulled her up. "Come on."

"Get the fuck off of me!" She said snatching away from me.

"Just go take the fucking test and stop being a damn brat all the time!"

"I'm not taking the test."

"Why the fuck not. Your mom was right when she said you were gaining weight even now looking at you, plus you're throwing up and shit."

"I'm not taking a test. There's no need."

"And why is that?"

"I already took one." She whispered.

"And?" She looked at me and darted her face down again. I grabbed her chin and lifted it up, and she was crying.

"You are, aren't you?"

She snatched away from me and slowly nodded her head. I shut my eyes and balled my fist up and brought them to my head. "FUCK!" I yelled out.

I heard her whimper and opened my eyes, and she was sitting on my couch with her head in her hands crying.

"Tri man, fuck. How did this shit happen?"

"You know how. You're not an idiot you know how babies are made."

"I thought you were on birth control man."

She hopped up and jumped in my face. "Don't fucking put this on me! I told your dumbass to wear a condom and you didn't so don't act like this is all on me."

"So, is there a possibility its anyone else's?" I knew how Trina was. She was me in female form.

I never saw the slap coming and I grabbed my face and mugged her.

"Fuck you, Duke! Don't sit here like I'm some fucking hoe who's trying to trap you; shit just happened with us and the second time you came on to me. So, don't play me for some common ass hoe!"

I took a deep breath and stepped back and looked at her. She was beautiful even with her tear stained face. She was glowing, and the small pudge from my baby made her even more beautiful.

I walked back over to her and grabbed her by her waist and leaned my head down, so my forehead was touching hers.

"Your right I'm sorry. I'm out of line, and it takes two. We're going to get through this and we're going to raise our baby together." I kissed her.

"What about Nike? He's not going to be okay with this."

I took a deep breath and looked at her. She was right Nike was going to be pissed, but no one was going to come in between me raising my child.

"We'll worry about that later okay. He'll be pissed but what can he do?"

She stepped away from me and looked down.

"What if I don't want to keep it?" I had to double take to make sure I heard her correctly.

"Yo, what the fuck did you just say?"

"I'm not sure if I want to have this baby. I'm not ready and to have you as my child's father I don't know how I feel about it."

"What the fuck is that supposed to mean."

"I grew up with you Duke; I know how you are. Do you think you'd be a good father? You're reckless as fuck and only care about yourself."

90

I had to close my eyes and remember this was my best friend's sister, someone I had grown to care about above the sister level, and someone who was now my child's mother.

"So, I'm not good enough to be your child's father? Who is? That bitch nigga you were at the mall."

"This doesn't have anything to do with Ashur. Plus weren't you at the mall with some bitch."

"I don't have another man's baby in my fucking stomach."

"Yeah well, in a few days it won't be in there, so it doesn't matter."

I walked up on her and quickly grabbed her jaws and squeezed them together. I felt myself slipping into the black place.

"Don't fucking play with me Trina. I care about you deeper than just being my nigga's sister. But you get rid of my fucking baby, and I'm going to forget all that. I'm not fucking playing with you." I let her go and turned and walked towards my stairs.

"So that's it? You just say what you have to say walk away."

"You can take it how you want. Now either leave or come up stairs and let me fuck some sense in you." I didn't wait on her because I knew Trina, she was about to make me make her remember who the fuck I am.

CHAPTER 17

*N*oni
    I was at Verizon. I had gotten rid of my phone and got a new one with a new number. Deshawn was still texting me, and I refused to tell King he was still pissed about my breakdown I had. So, I refused to add fuel to the fire. Besides Deshawn didn't know where I lived, and he had never met any of my family besides my sister.

After I sent my number to the appropriate people, I went to my school so I could purchase my books for the semester that started in two weeks. I was excited because after I finished these last few years I was officially done with school.

I was leaving the book store when I bumped into something hard. I stumbled, and a pair of hands grabbed me. I looked up and swallowed.

This man was gorgeous with is milk chocolate skin, he had dreads that were currently pulled in a bun, and he was cocky built.

"I'm sorry I wasn't watching where I was going," I said.

"No problem, it's not every day a beautiful woman bumps into you." I blushed.

"I should get going."

"Damn, I can't even get your name." I laughed a little and looked at his dark eyes and then looked at his full lips and beard outlining it.

"Shonni. And you are?" I asked cocking my head to the side?

"Shamar." I nodded and gave her another look over. "You go to school here?"

"Yeah, I'm finishing up my masters here. How about you?" I shifted my weight to the side waiting for him to answer. He was so handsome with a rugged look to him.

"Nah, I'm here picking my brother up." My phone vibrated, and I looked at the screen and seen it was King.

"Look I have to go. I'm sorry again for bumping into you."

"Can I get yo number, maybe we can grab something to eat."

I played with the idea but then thought back to how mad King got when I mention dating.

"Right now, I have a situation going on with my son's father, so I don't think that's wise."

"Well, how about you take mine and if that situation ever breaks call me."

I smiled, and he read off his number, and I saved it and said goodbye and headed towards my car. When I got to the parking lot, I got to my car and went to open the door, and I heard my name. I turned around and jumped. I had to double take because I swear I Deshawn was looking right at me smiling. I closed my eyes and looked again, and he was gone. I needed to get a grip, Deshawn isn't here, and there was no reason for me to be scared anymore.

My phone started going off again and I looked and it was King calling me again. I wasn't in the mood to talk to him. I was still shaken up so instead of answering I headed to Trina's house, I know she had told Duke about the pregnancy, and since then he wouldn't let her leave his sight.

I got to Trina's and knocked on the door I stood there waiting for her to come to the door.

"Hey boo." I said soon as she opened the door.

"Hey what are you doing here?" She asked.

"Damn, I can't just come visit you anymore." She rolled her eyes

"Of course, you can but you never just pop up." She yawned and stretched, and I looked at her rounding belly.

"Tired?"

"Girl yes, me and Duke stayed up all night arguing and fucking."

I laughed because sadly that sounded just like them. "Why?"

"He wants to tell my mom and brother that I'm pregnant and that it's his baby."

"Okay? What's wrong with that?"

"Bitch my mom might understand but Kingston ass definitely won't!"

"Your grown Trina he doesn't have much of a say so in what you do!"

"Have you met my brother?"

"Bitch I have a baby by him."

"And you see how he is with you!"

"That's different I have his son, of course, he's gonna act like he has no damn common sense, but I don't pay his ass any attention."

"Yeah, okay, that's why yo ass is still at his house. We know who wears the pants in y'all relationship."

I blew a breath out. "Bitch, there is no relationship. Besides we're talking about you, not me."

"I just don't want to cause any unnecessary drama." She ran her hand over her face, and I laughed she looked just like King when she did that.

"We're all getting together for Sunday dinner, this weekend, right? Why not tell them then?"

She bit her lip like she was in deep thought. "I don't know if I'm ready for that. I don't know if me and Duke are together or not plus, I know he's got to be still doing his own thing."

"Trina, take it from someone whose done this alone. It sucks if you have a man that wants this child and wants to be there embrace it."

She began to rub her stomach, and I felt sorry for her. She looked so scared, and this wasn't Trina. Trina wasn't scared of anything, she was such a free spirit and to see her at the point where she looked defeated broke my heart.

I walked over to her and hugged her, and she began to cry. "I just don't want to be alone in this. What if my brother doesn't accept it, you know he's my rock, Noni."

"Your brother loves you, as long as Duke doesn't mistreat you he's gonna deal with it." She didn't say anything though. I know she was in a fucked-up situation, but she couldn't let that stop her from being happy. King was gonna be pissed, but it was something he would have to learn to deal with.

$\sim$

Once I finally got home, I knew King was gonna be pissed I hadn't answered his phone call all morning but after thinking I saw Deshawn I just wasn't in the mood.

I got out and slowly walked to the door. Soon as I reached for the knob the door was snatch opened, and there stood King with a scowl on his handsome face.

"Why the fuck aren't you answering my phone calls?" He yelled.

I jumped and looked around before answering.

"I was talking to Trina. I'm sorry."

"So, you been at Trina's this whole time and couldn't pick up the phone? Speaking of phones, why did you get a new number?"

I hesitated for a minute because I couldn't tell him the truth.

"I went to the phone place, then to The University to get my books then- wait why am I explaining myself to you."

"What the fuck do you mean why? It takes two seconds to answer the fucking phone! I don't even know why I'm still trying with you!"

I stared at him and I began to feel bad. I know King was only looking out for me. Even though he doesn't know about the texts I had been getting, he knows how paranoid I am that Deshawn will find me.

He looked so frustrated and that made me feel even worse. I know he wants nothing more but for us to work our shit out but I was scared. I know it's been some years since everything happened with us but I didn't know how to let the hurt go. I loved King and I want to be with him, but I've built a defensive wall against him that it's hard for me to let it down.

"I'm sorry, your right. I could have answered, I fucked up."

"I don't know what to do anymore Noni. I want this to work, but I'm not about to keep kissing your ass for some shit I did years ago."

I didn't know what to say, so I didn't say anything. I pushed past him and walked into the house and halfway up the stairs, I heard the door slam. Silently I cried walking to the room I was staying in. I know if I didn't get my shit together I was going to lose King, and that was the last thing I wanted.

CHAPTER 18

Nike

I pulled up to Taliyah's house and sighed. She had been begging me to spend some time with her and I was brushing her off because I thought after the night Noni broke down we would be getting somewhere, but I see I was wrong.

I meant it when I told her I was tired of kissing her ass. As bad as I wanted to be a family with her and my son, I was over the shit just the same. If she wanted to co-parent and raise our son apart then I would have to give her that.

I got out the car and walked up to the door and knocked on it. Taliyah opened the door in a pink satin robe and heels. I bit my lip and looked her up and down.

"Hey come in." She said turning and walking back into her house.

Her ass was hanging out the bottom of the robe and I know today was the day I had to slide in her. I hadn't had no pussy in a few weeks trying to wait on Noni, but I wasn't worried about hat shit anymore.

I followed behind her and walked in and sat on her couch. "I'm happy you finally had time for me." She said sitting on my lap.

I smirked and looked at her. "Oh yeah?"

She nodded and turned to straddle me. I put my hands on her waist and she started slowly moving her hips in my lap. My hand slid under robe and inside the panties she had on and I rubbed my finger over her slit. She wrapped arms around my neck and leaned forward and I began kissing on her neck.

I began thumbing her clit and she let out a moan and started grinding on my finger. Her shit was starting to soak my pants and I slipped a finger in her. I was expecting her shit to grip my finger but it just barely did that.

I told her to lift up, and when she did I stood up and grabbed the condom out my back pocket and pulled my basketball shorts and boxers down.

"Bend over the couch for me." I whispered. She did as she was told and I pulled her panties ripping them and tossed them to the side. I opened the condom and slid it on my dick and got behind her. I gripped my dick and rubbed it up and down the outside of her opening.

"Put it in baby." She whined.

I smirked and did as she asked and shoved my dick in her. "FUCK NIKE" She yelled out as I started moving in and out of her.

Her shit still wasn't gripping my shit like I wanted and it was pissing me off because her ass was throwing it back and yelling like I was trying to kill her.

"Your dick feels so good baby."

I slapped her ass and started moving faster, and tried to go deeper. "Oh yeah?" I asked.

"Yes baby, beat this pussy up!" I grabbed the back of her neck and told her to throw her as back faster, but she put her hand on my stomach trying to stop me.

"Wait baby you're too deep." But I wasn't paying her any attention. I slapped her hand away and tried to focus on my nut.

"I'm cumming Nike!" She yelled and creamed all over my dick. She collapsed soon as she came and I was even more pissed.

"We ain't done so get up." I said.

"I can't take any more baby."

She had me fucked up if she thought I wasn't about to cum. If I didn't want to leave with blue balls I would have bounced and left her and her mediocre pussy. I sat down next to her and grabbed her and pulled her on top of me. I shoved her down on my girth and started to move her hips in the rhythm I needed her to go. I let her waist go, and she began bouncing up and down.

Even though her shit wasn't gripping my dick like I needed it too, she was still riding the fuck out of me. I began humping her from below and she announced she was cumming again, and I knew that if I didn't get my nut now it was over. I grabbed her waist and pictured the one thing I knew could make me cum.

"Fuck Nike!" She yelled and soon as she started cumming I was following suit.

❦

I walked in my house and Noni and KJ was sitting on the couch watching TV. She glanced at me and then back at the TV. I felt guilty because I had just fucked Taliyah and was now coming to the house I was currently sharing with the love of my life and my son.

I walked straight upstairs to my bedroom and stripped out my clothes and headed to my bathroom to shower.

I put on a pair of boxers and grey joggers and walked out my room and back downstairs to talk to Noni. When I got downstairs I seen bags by the door and Noni came down stairs carrying more.

"What's going on?" I asked, but she didn't answer. She didn't respond. She pushed past me and walked outside and I watched her put her bags in her car. She came back in and picked up some more and she still didn't say anything. When she got to the last of her bags I was pissed because she had yet to speak. I grabbed her when she started towards KJ and she turned and looked at me and she was crying.

"What are you doing?" I asked her. She looked down and my hand on her and snatched away.

"I'm going home." She said.

"No, the fuck you're not."

"Look I'm not about to stay here and you're out fucking other bitches! You get mad whenever I mention myself with another nigga, but you walk your ugly ass in here smelling like you just crawled out some bitch's pussy! Fuck you!" By this time, she stopped crying and was looking at me in pure disgust.

"I wasn't fucking no other bitch Noni, and if I was so what, it's not like your trying to fuck with me."

She swallowed, turned and looked at KJ.

"How am I supposed to know you won't hurt me again?" She asked lowly.

I grabbed her by her waist and pulled her into me and looked down at her. "You just got to trust me. I love the fuck out of you Noni and I want to make this work, but you have to meet me halfway." I kissed her forehead and stepped back.

"I'm going to give yo space, because I see that you're not in the right head space to deal with me. But I can't wait for you forever."

"Does she mean anything to you, she whispered so low I barely heard her, do you love her?"

I smirked and stared at her for a minute. "How the fuck am I supposed to love her when I'm caught up with this stubborn ass, thick, big booty girl."

She laughed and turned and walked to the couch and picked up KJ. She began walking towards me and stopped in front of me. I grabbed KJ and turned and started towards the door. I stopped at it and turned and looked at her, but she wouldn't meet my eye. She continued out the door and to her car, and I followed. I put KJ in the car after kissing him on the forehead and the turned and faced her. I pulled her into me and bent down and kissed her, slipping my tongue in her mouth. My hands found her ass and she moaned in my mouth but I pulled back.

No matter if I wanted to take it there I couldn't disrespect her like that, not after I just been in Taliyah.

"Call me when you get home and settled in." I said. She slowly nodded and got in her car and I stuck my hands in my pocket and watched her start the car and reverse the driveway.

CHAPTER 19

*D*uke

I looked at my phone reading the dumb shit Trina had sent me and locked my phone, not even bothering to respond. She was refusing to tell her brother she was pregnant with my baby and I was sick of her shit.

I cared for Trina and I felt like she balanced me out, but if she couldn't stand up to her brother then I could never be with her. I shook my head just as Farrah walked out her bathroom in a towel and sat next to me. She was leaving in the morning and wanted to spend some time with me before she did.

"Hey, you okay?" She asked.

I nodded and put my phone on her dresser. "Yeah, just some dumb shit going on. Nothing you need to worry about." I grabbed her and pulled her into my lap and she smiled. If Farrah didn't have to travel so much or I would make her my girl. She never nagged me and always made sure I was good. Even when she was gone she always hit me up and checked on me.

She was a beautiful girl, her golden skin always glowed and reminded me of honey. She had golden blond hair that complimented her skin even more. Her big, light brown eyes fit her round face and she had freckles across her nose. She was around 5'6 and was toned as fuck due to her training every day. Her breast was the size of tennis balls, but her ass was like a basketball. I loved watching it as I hit her from the back.

Even though I was beginning to feel Trina, I couldn't lie and say I didn't have an attraction to Farrah.

"I'm sad I have to leave in the morning." She pouted, wrapping her arms my neck.

"Shit, me too, you got some good ass pussy." I bit my lip and then laughed as she hit me.

"I'm serious Duke. I really enjoy spending time with you."

"Well how about we make it last while you here."

"Are you going to come visit me when I leave?"

I looked her in her eyes and took a deep breath. "I don't know Farrah I got a lot of shit going on right now that I need to figure out, and it wouldn't be fair to drag you into it."

She didn't dig any deeper, she just nodded her head and I was happy. Farrah was a great catch and I was dog ass nigga. We had built a genuine friendship, so I would never give her hope that we would be more than what we are now, especially since I wasn't sure what was gonna happen with Trina.

Instead of continuing any conversation, I reach over and grabbed and condom and prepared fucked her ass like it was the last time.

❦

I hadn't seen or talked to Trina in two days, so when I pulled into Momma T's for Sunday dinner and seen her car my heart started racing. I wasn't sure how today was going to go, but I was mentally prepared for the bullshit.

I walked into the house and into the dining room where everyone was sitting. "What's up yall." I gave Momma T a kiss on the cheek and sat down.

"What's up Noni," I said looking at her. She smiled and waved. "Where yo man at?"

She balled her face up and shrugged her shoulders. "What's up Tri?" I looked at her and licked my lips. My baby was filling her out good as fuck, it made me want to slide up in her in front of everyone right now.

"Soon ask Kingston gets his ass here we can eat." Soon as Momma T said that King came in and we all got a shock of our lives. He walked in with a female. No one said a word, everyone was looking from Noni to Kingston and the girl.

"Kingston who the fuck is this?" Trina yelled.

"Trina, watch your mouth, Momma T said. But she's right, who the fuck is this?"

"Yall rude, he said laughing, this is Taliyah. Taliyah that's my momma, everyone calls her Momma T, and that's my sister Trina."

"You can call me Mrs. Tolliver." Momma T said mugging both of them.

I swear Nike ain't have it all upstairs. I looked over at Noni, and the hurt was written all over her face. She was so in love with my boy, and his ass kept fucking her over.

He grabbed the Taliyah's hand and led her to the opposite side of the table so that they were sitting directly in front of Noni and their son.

"Hey, dad!" KJ yelled oblivious to the tension in the room right now.

"What's up son." He stood up and reached his fist out and KJ dapped him out.

"What's up Noni." He said looked at her.

She didn't respond, she grabbed her phone and focused on it.

"Awh, is that your son?" Taliyah said.

"Didn't my nephew just call him dad?" Trina asked with a blank look.

Noni chuckled but didn't say anything out loud. "I was just making sure." She said and rolled her eyes

"Bitch roll them again and I'll-"

"You ain't gone do shit but sit there." I said and she mugged me.

"Nike are you going to introduce me to everyone else."

"Yeah, my bad. That's my brother Duke, that's my son KJ, and that's his mother, Noni."

"It's Shonni." She said not looking up from her phone.

"Who the fuck you over there texting?" He asked he cut his eyes at her, and Taliyah did the same to him.

I laughed because Noni didn't even respond to him. "Can we eat I'm starving," Trina said rubbing her stomach. She looked good as fuck with her hair pulled up in a ponytail showing off her now chubby face. I noticed she had on a big ass t-shirt that hid her stomach and that pissed me off.

"Why you wearing that big ass shirt Tri?" She gave me a deadly stare and ignored me.

"We're just waiting for your dad to get here." Momma T said.

"So KJ how old are you?" Taliyah asked.

"KJ, don't talk to strangers, son." Noni said still not looking up from her phone. Taliyah sucked her teeth, and the rest of the table laughed including Nike.

"I don't think it was that funny," Taliyah said turning and looking at him. He shrugged his shoulders and chuckled again.

"Mommy, is she a thot?" KJ tried to whisper. The whole table started laughing again. This time Noni set her phone down and looked at him.

"What do you know about thots, little boy?" She asked.

"I heard you tell Aunt Trina that daddy won't stop messing with thots." He said shrugging his shoulders.

Noni turned beat red and cleared her throat. "Just don't say that word anymore." She picked her phone back up and began pecking at it again.

"So where did you come from?" Momma T asked looking at Taliyah.

"Ma, come on man." Nike groaned.

"What you bring some random ass women in my house I think I deserve to know."

"Lauri leave that boy alone." Nike's and Trina's dad said to

Momma T, walking in and kissing her cheek. She rolled her eyes but didn't say anything else.

We finally began to eat, and what was usually a fun filled dinner was awkward as hell. Trina and Momma T kept throwing shots at Taliyah, and Noni was quiet as a mouse. The only ones that had an actual conversation was Nike, KJ, Mr. Tolliver, and I.

"I have an announcement to make!" Trina said once everyone was done eating. Everyone turned and looked at her and she looked at me and I nodded my head. She grabbed the bottom of her shirt and pulled it up.

"Aye, we don't want to see that." Nike yelled.

She sucked her teeth. "Shut up, I have a shirt on under this." She lifted the bigger t-shirt she had on up and she had a crop top on. She stood up and Momma T's hand went to her mouth.

"I knew it." She whispered.

"Yo, what the fuck is wrong with your stomach?" Nike's dumbass said.

"Baby she's pregnant, congratulations." Taliyah said smiling.

"Aye, shut the fuck up." Nike said mugging her.

"Watch your mouth son, Mr. Tolliver said. Who's the dad Trina?"

She was quiet and just when I was about to speak up she did.

"I don't know." She said lowly.

I felt a dagger go through my heart. I know she didn't just say she didn't know.

"Say that again." Nike said.

"I had a one-night stand and the condom broke. I don't remember his name, I was real drunk." She was avoiding eye contact with me and right there and then I knew Trina and I could never be together.

"How far are you?" Her mom said.

"Almost four months, I got pregnant around Duke's party."

"Y'all I'm about to head out." I said standing up. I said my goodbyes and kissed Noni and Momma T on the cheek, and went out to my car and headed to my favorite place, King of Diamonds.

CHAPTER 20

Deshawn
I had been keeping my eyes on Shonni since I got her address, and I was like a kid in a candy store when she finally showed up.

After seeing her bitch ass baby daddy, I was more than determined to get her and take her ass back to Atlanta. She had gotten her number changed. Every time I tried to call her or text her the number came up disconnected. No matter, I had following her and I know very soon she'd be mines again.

I was tired of the little games she was playing and when we got home, I was going to beat her ass so bad she'd never run away again. Noni knew I loved her. If she didn't make me so mad, and stop doing stupid shit then I wouldn't have to hit her.

Then her fucking son was annoying as shit. All he wanted to do was be stuck up her ass all day. I barely got any alone time with her, and then she complained and shot me down when I said I wanted her to have my baby. I don't know what made her think I would be okay with raising her bastard son, and she didn't want to give me my own. I should have been gotten rid of him, that's where I fucked up at.

The day I seen Noni at her school I know she noticed me and I was surprised she didn't have her nigga looking for me it felt so good seeing her. She still looked good as fuck. It had been a little over a year since she left me and if it wasn't for Facebook, I wouldn't have known where she was at.

I was prepared to make my presence known to her soon. But first I had to deal with her baby daddy. I pulled up to the house Evelynn was stashed at, and got out and walked over the door. I knocked and it took her a few minutes but she finally answered.

"Change of plans." I said pushing past her than turning and looking at her.

"I told you, Kingston forgave me, I'm out your crazy as plot to get that bitch back." She put her hands on her hips, and I laughed and walked over to her.

I back handed her, and she went flying on the floor. "Who the fuck are you talking to Evelynn? Do your dumbass really believe that nigga is going to let you get away with busting his son's head open."

She looked at me like the dumbass she is, holding her face. "Did you meet up with that nigga?" She shook her head.

"He told me something came up when I talked to him."

"Get him to meet up with you."

She slowly stood up, still holding her face and stared at me. "Why are you changing your mind now?"

"Because Shonni isn't gonna leave that nigga. If you can keep him distracted, then I can get her to forgive me and come back home, to Atlanta."

"Shawn, do you hear yourself. I don't think that will work." I smiled and took a step closer to her.

"Well good thing you're not being paid to think. Get him to meet up with you and when he agrees let me know." I pushed past her again and headed out the door.

Since it was time for me to put my plan in motion for Kingston to get out the way I decided to start working on my plan to get Shonni back.

I drove to a local flower shop and grabbed 12 white Lilies, they were Noni's favorite and headed to her school. I had followed her enough to know her classes were coming to an end for the day.

I pulled into the parking garage and was happy to see a parking spot next to Noni's car. I waited for about fifteen minutes, and she strutted her sexy ass towards her car, and I hopped out of mine and called her name, and she jumped and slowly turned around.

"Wh-wha-what are you doing here?" She asked looking around.

I walked closer to her, and she backed away. "I'm not here to fight you. I only want to talk. I miss you, and I want you to come back to Atlanta with me." I went to hand her the flowers, and she smacked them out my hand, and I bit the back of my jaw.

"How did you even find me? I'm not going with you, Deshawn." She turned, and I grabbed her turning her around.

"You know I don't fucking like you turning your back on me Noni." I gritted.

"Let me go, Deshawn. Please leave, I don't want to be with you anymore. I ran away from you for a reason!"

"To be with your punk ass baby daddy?" Her eyes widened, and she tried to snatch away from me.

"How do you know I've been seeing him?" She asked.

"Come on Noni; I know everything."

"Well if you know everything, you know my baby dad is crazy, and if you don't leave me alone, he's going to kill you." She began laughing, and I felt myself getting hot. Before I could stop myself, my hand connected with her face and it went back.

"Fuck, do you see what you made me do again Noni? I came here to have a peaceful conversation with you, and you made me do this shit to you!" I looked down at her; she was on the ground crying holding her eye.

"This is why I left you! I'm not your fucking punching bag!" I looked around, and seen people began walking in the parking garage.

I bent down and grabbed her by her neck and whispered, "You will come back to Atlanta with me, I don't care who I have to kill to get you back home, I'm not leaving Miami without you." I kissed her cheek, stood up, and backed up and got in my car and drove off and decided to lay low for a while.

CHAPTER 21

*T*rina

I had fucked up royally with Duke, and I felt like shit. I saw the hurt on his face when I told my family that I didn't know who the father of my baby was. I didn't mean to lie, I was gonna tell the truth, but before I could stop myself, the lie spilled out.

Duke refused to speak to me, he came to my doctor's appointment and didn't speak one word. It hurt me, but what hurt me more is that I had hurt him. No matter how much we argued, Duke was very supportive if I called him because my cravings he would stop what he was doing a go grab it. He would stay the night and rub my stomach at night, and he never missed an appointment.

I felt like shit because I had fallen in love with Duke and I did him wrong. I wanted to fix it, but I wasn't sure if I was ready to face my brother and tell him the truth. I cried for two days straight because Duke ignored my phone calls and responded with texts, telling me, not to call if it's not about the baby.

I couldn't eat or sleep, and I know that wasn't good for the baby, but I couldn't handle what I was feeling. I was sitting on my couch, listening to *Avenue by H.E.R,* blast through my Bluetooth speaker, and there was a knock on the door. I groaned and stayed where I was at, hoping they would go away.

I grabbed my phone and turned up the volume because I didn't want to be bothered and whoever was at the door wasn't getting the picture. I turned the music off and grabbed my phone and tried to call Duke for what seemed like millionth time. He was really starting to piss me off; I'm pregnant with his child. What if something was wrong.

Whoever was knocking on the door must have gotten the hint because they stopped knocking. I put my phone on the couch next to me and laid my head back and closed my eyes. A few minutes later my door opened, and I opened one eye and seen my mom standing in front of me with one hand on her hip.

"Little girl I know you heard me knocking on the door." She said.

"Mom I'm not in the mood for company right now," I said closing my eyes back.

"Trina, I'm not your brother or father that little-spoiled ass attitude don't work with me."

I felt my self getting pissed off. Why couldn't she just leave me alone?

"I know you just went to the doctors. How's the baby?"

I ignored her because I didn't want to talk about the baby because my baby's father wouldn't talk to me. I continued to lay there hoping she would leave but she didn't she sat down next to me. I laid on her shoulder and started to cry. This was always our routine when I was younger and upset. I'd give everyone the silent treatment, but soon as my mom got near me, I would break down.

"I lied at dinner." I finally said. But she didn't say anything she just rubbed my back.

"I'm pregnant with Duke's baby."

"I figured that." She finally said.

I popped my head off her shoulder and looked at her, and she laughed.

"You don't think I don't notice the glances y'all be giving each other or how damn awkward y'all all around one another now.

Plus, when you announced your pregnancy you couldn't keep your eyes off that damn boy."

"Why didn't you say something?"

"It wasn't for me to say something. That was something you had to do."

"Yeah, well now he's pissed at me because I lied and he won't talk to me." I was ready for this pregnancy to be over because I was always crying.

"Why did you lie?"

"Nike would kill us if he found out we messed around behind his back! I screeched.

"So the fuck what if yo brother is mad Trina, you are about to bring a damn baby in the world. Who gives a fuck if what Kingston thinks, you have to raise this baby with Duke, not him."

"But he's my best friend, what if he's mad at me."

"I told yo brother he spoiled you too damn much. Trina when you create a child the man you chose to do that with comes before everyone but that child. Now, yes, your brother is probably going to shit bricks and him and Duke might even fight, she stopped and laughed.

But at the end of the day, your brother just wants you happy."

"I think I love him, mom," I whispered and looked at my hands.

"So tell him that, yo ass ain't never been scared to speak your mind. Why are you now?"

"What if he doesn't feel the same? I don't want him to feel like he's forced to be with me because I'm pregnant."

"I swear I think someone dropped you on your head as a baby and didn't tell me. I see how that light skinned boy looks at you Trina; I don't even know how your brother hasn't seen it."

"He won't answer my phone calls!"

"You hurt him and probably killed his ego. Give him some time."

I started getting cramps in my stomach and began rubbing my hand in a circular motion.

"Are you okay?" My mom asked.

"Yeah, just a little discomfort." I continued to rub on my stomach.

TAY MO'NAE

"You're getting yourself too worked up. I'm going to go into the kitchen and see what you have to make you something to eat. You just sit here and calm down." I nodded and laid my head back, and my phone began to ring.

I picked it up and looked at it and saw it was Duke. I smiled and answered.

"Duke I'm sorry!" I said soon as I answered, but he said nothing.

"Duke?" I pulled the phone back and made sure he was there.

I figured he had butt dialed me and was about to hang up until I heard his voice.

"Look I came here to leave my stress, please don't add to it," He said.

"Your right I'm sorry baby." The girl said.

Baby? I felt my face ball up and pressed the phone tighter against my ear.

"If you're sorry, come ride daddy's dick."

"Yesss daddy, like this?"

She began moaning and yelling out his name. "Fuck Farrah just like that girl." Farrah? That's the bitch he was at the mall with.

Tears began forming in my eyes again but wouldn't l let them fall. "I love you, Duke!" "Shit get up and turn around," Duke demanded.

"You love me huh? Show me throw that ass back and make me cum baby." I heard their skin slapping against one another, and I literally felt my heart tearing.

"DUKE!" I yelled

"DUKE I SWEAR TO GOD!"

"What the fuck is that?" I heard him shifting around, and I continued to yell out his name.

"Fuck, Trina?" He said.

"Are you fucking serious!?" I yelled, and my mom came running out the kitchen.

"What's the matter? Why are you yelling?" She said.

But I was too amped up to answer.

"You told me that bitch wasn't shit to worry about, but you're still fucking her!"

114

"Trina, calm down let me explain baby."

"Fuck you! I know I made the right decision not telling my brother your dirty ass was my baby's father!" The cramping I had earlier came back, and I hunched over dropping the phone.

"Trina, what's wrong? Are you okay? My mom rushed over to me and grabbed me.

"Mom something's not right." I was gripping my stomach, praying I wasn't losing my baby right now.

"We're going to the hospital." She said.

My mom picked my phone up and then ran into the kitchen, I guess to turn off whatever she started to cook.

"Duke calm down, just come to the hospital when you land, okay?" My mom had told Duke, still on the phone with him.

"Land? Where the fuck is he?" I yelled still gripping my stomach.

"Trina shut the fuck up and calm down." My mom yelled

"No! Tell him since he's taking trips with that bitch he could stay with her." She didn't respond she grabbed me instead and helped me to the door.

I was balling my eyes out by the point, and I began to get real hot. My vision blurred and then everything went black.

CHAPTER 22

*D*uke
I was so fucked up over what Trina had done that I spent probably close to a thousand dollars at the strip club. Every day since Sunday I'd handle business and then go there, more than likely end up fucking one of them.

Trina had definitely knocked me off my square, and though she apologized, I wasn't ready to accept it. Until she told her family who the real father of her child was, I had nothing to say to her, outside our baby.

I had currently just landed in Texas, a couple of days ago I was talking to Farrah, and she invited me to come stay the weekend with her after hearing my fucked mood.

Once I was in my rental, I plugged her address in my GPS and headed her way. Soon as I got to her place and knocked on the door, she was on me, kissing me and wrapping her arms around me. I dropped my bags and I bent down and picked her up and her legs went immediately around me.

"You have no idea how bad I want your dick in me right now." She said.

She didn't have to let me know twice. I walked into her house and closed the door not caring my bags were still on the porch.

I turned and slammed her back into the wall. While I kept her supported with one hand, I worked my pants and boxers down with the other. She had was only wearing a thong and t-shirt, so I slid the thong to the side and shoved her down on my dick. Her mouth gasped in an O, but I wasn't worried, Farrah was always a champ in the bedroom, and I needed to release some aggression.

I began pounding her down harder and she gripped my neck tighter.

I felt her pussy contract on my dick, and her body began to shake.

"Shit Duke I'm coming." She yelled.

I felt myself about to cum, and I remembered I didn't have a rubber on. Soon as I feel her cream cum on my dick, I hurried and lifted her and came on her stomach.

I put her down on the ground and asked her where the bathroom was. When she directed me towards the restroom, I walked in and fell against the door.

I was fucking up, the only bitch I ever went raw in was Trina, and she was supposed to be the only one. Farrah was cool, but I didn't know what she did when I wasn't around, and I wasn't trying to get her ass pregnant either.

This shit with Trina had me fucking up big time. I looked down at my limp dick and seen her juice coating it and shook my head. I grabbed some paper towels she had sitting by the sink and wet them and washed my dick off and put it back in my boxers. I pulled my pants up and grabbed my ringing phone and seen it was Trina. I still wasn't in the mood to talk to her, so I ignored the call and headed back into the living room.

I ended up staying in Texas an extra day because Farrah had begged me to. She had gotten extra clingy the four days I've been here. Not to mention she got an attitude every time she saw Trina call, which I don't know why I wasn't answering and Farrah wasn't my girl.

I know what I was doing was wrong. Trina was pregnant with my child, but I didn't have shit to say to her until she told her brother the truth.

I was currently in the shower, Farrah and I have been fucking all weekend, and I was drained for the first time. This girl had the biggest sexual appetite. She always been wild in the bedroom but spending four days straight with her definitely brought out another side of her.

I washed up and got out the shower and grabbed my towel and dried off. I wrapped the towel around my waist and opened the bathroom door and headed down the hall to Farrah's room.

"Why the fuck you touching my phone, Farrah?" I asked when I walked in.

"It kept ringing, so I was going to silence it." She said still holding it.

"Put my shit back where you got it, and don't touch it again."

I turned around to grab my clothes out my bag.

"I just don't understand why she keeps calling you! Every time I'm trying to spend time with you she's fucking calling."

"Farrah, I don't know what the fuck is going on with you, but you better fix that shit. You don't have no right to question who calls my damn phone."

I turned around and looked at her with a smirk. She was look good as fuck with the scowl she was currently sporting.

I dropped my clothes and walked over to the bed and grabbed her.

"Look I came here to leave my stress, please don't add to it."

"Your right baby. I'm sorry."

I reached over and grabbed a condom off her night stand. "If you're sorry, come ride daddy's dick."

She bit her lip and walked over to me and slowly sat on my hard dick. Her shit gripped my dick tight as fuck, had me ready to bust soon as she slid down.

"Yesss daddy, she said, like this?"

She began bouncing and winding her hips, and I grabbed hold of her waist and began matching her rhythm. "Duke you feel so good, baby."

"Fuck Farrah just like that girl."

"I love you, Duke." My dick almost went limp. I knew I would have to cut Farrah off for a while after this. I cared for her, but I didn't love her.

"Shit get up and turn around," I said tapping her leg, and she did as I asked.

She bent over the bed, and I shoved myself inside of her. "You love me huh? Show me throw that ass back and make me cum baby."

Farrah began throwing it back matching my speed, and I was getting ready to bust when I heard my name. I thought I was hearing things, so I got my rhythm back and grabbed her neck and started drilling into her.

"DUKE I SWEAR TO GOD." I stopped and turned my head towards the direction the voice was coming from. "What the fuck is that?"

"Duke, what the fuck?" Farrah whispered turning her head. I ignored her and seen my phone was lit up with a phone call displaying. I pulled out of Farrah and walked over to my phone and the color drained from my face.

Fuck Trina? I said more to myself, seeing her contact displayed on the screen. I picked the phone up and placed it on my ear.

"ARE YOU FUCKING SERIOUS?" She yelled, and I pulled the phone from my ear and seen she had been on the phone for going on ten minutes.

"You told me that bitch wasn't shit to worry about, but you're still fucking her!" I didn't even know how to get myself out this shit, how the fuck did she get on the phone?

"Trina, calm down let me explain baby."

"Fuck you! I know I made the right decision not telling my brother your dirty ass was my baby's father!" I was about to cuss her dumbass out when I heard her groan.

"Trina, what's wrong? Are you okay?" My heart dropped I looked over a Farrah, and she was texting on her fucking phone unbothered that I was about to lose my fucking mind.

"Trina, Trina! I yelled. I heard someone talking and something about a hospital.

"Duke, she's getting really bad stomach pains, I'm about to take her to get looked at." Momma T said.

"Fuck, man, Momma T I'm sorry. I just wanted to teach her lesson; I swear I didn't want this to happen. I'm about to catch a flight from Texas right now."

"Duke, calm down, just come to the hospital when you land, okay?" I heard Trina yelling in the background, and Momma T was trying to get her calmed down.

"Trina, wake up! Baby come on. Duke, she passed out hurry!" Before I could answer the phone hung up.

I started banging my fist against my head and felt tears forming in my eyes, which hasn't happened since my mom died. If I lost my child or Trina, I'd lose my mind.

"Are we going to finish or not?" Farrah asked like she didn't just hear my conversation.

"Are you fucking stupid? I know you just heard my phone conversation? I have to get to back to Atlanta and check on my baby and its mother.

She rolled her eyes, and I mugged her and walked over to my bag and began getting dressed. Farrah was cut off after this. Trina had just heard me fucking another bitch, even though she wasn't my girl, I would never disrespect her like that. I was rushing putting my clothes trying to figure out how Trina got on the phone and it hit me, Farrah. The stupid bitch had my phone right before we started fucking.

I turned and rushed to her and grabbed her by her neck and slammed her back on her bed. "Bitch, how the fuck did Trina get on the phone?" She began clawing at my hand and swinging trying to get me off her." She swung and got me in my nose, and I let her go and grabbed my nose.

"Are you fucking crazy?" She yelled.

I cut my eyes at her and took my shirt off and put it up to my nose. "How the fuck did Trina get on the phone. I'm not gonna ask you again."

"I called her." She said and shrugged.

"What the fuck do you mean you called her? How did you unlock my phone?"

"I watched you put your code in, and I wanted to tell her to stop fucking calling you so much." I threw my shirt and walked over to her and grabbed her by her neck again and lifted her up.

"Bitch lose my fucking number. If Trina loses my baby because the shit you pulled I'll kill you and that's on my unborn." I turned and tossed her, and she hit the wall and slid down gasping for air and holding her shoulder. I grabbed my phone and bloody shirt and put it in my bag. I finished getting dress and took one more look at Farrah and grabbed my bag and headed out the door.

CHAPTER 23

*E*velynn
I was tired of hiding, and I wanted to see Nike, some girl had answered the phone one day when I called, and since then my calls have been going straight to voicemail.

I went into the garage of the house I was staying and got into my car. I was tired of Shawn telling me what to do, and I had to warn Nike about him. I was taking a risk because Shawn could have been right and he could have still been mad at me for pushing his son, but I would never know if I didn't talk to him.

I headed in the direction of Deluxe Wheels, which was about an hour from where I was staying. I had been hiding out in Fort Lauderdale at my parent's second home that they hardly ever went to.

I pulled into Deluxe Wheels and grinned when I saw Nike's Maserati parked outside. I got out and switched into the shop like I owned it. I looked around when I entered and seen his office door open and strolled right past is receptionist that was yelling for me to stop and walked right in.

"You can't go in there!" She yelled.

Nike looked up and cut his eyes at me. "It's cool Janet; she can stay. Close the door on your way out." I smiled and walked over to his desk and sat in the chairs across from him. He leaned back and placed hands behind his head and glared at me.

I looked him over and admired his thick lips and his beard. Nike was so sexy, I knew from the first day I saw him he was meant to be mine.

"Well since your little bitch block me, I decided to make a trip." I said.

"Well if she blocked you, shouldn't that have told you something?" He said raising his eyebrow.

I stood up and strutted over to him. "When have I ever given a fuck about any female you fuck with Nike." I ran my hand over his crotch. I began having flashbacks of his thick dick inside of me.

"You miss this dick, don't you?" He asked me.

I nodded my head and began playing with his zipper.

"Shit, show me. Show daddy what that mouth do." I happily obligated and dropped down to my knees he turned and faced me. I unzipped his pants, and he leaned up a little pulling them down and pulled his dick out the slit of his boxers. I smiled Nike had the prettiest dick I had ever seen.

I eagerly grabbed his dick and put it in my mouth. I began bobbing my head up and down and pulled up and spit on it and run my hands up and down it before slipping it back in my mouth. I relaxed my throat and tried to take the whole thing in my mouth while I began massaging his balls. I started moving my hands around his dick in a circular motion and moved my head up and down sucking him like a vacuum.

Nike grabbed my hair and began forcing me to take him deeper in my mouth. I began to gag and tried to pull up, but he wouldn't let up. My eyes began to water, and he snatched my head back and began stroking his dick and busted all in my face.

"Nike, what the fuck!" I yelled.

He didn't say anything back though. He tucked his dick back in his pants and stood up and snatched me up by my hair pulling me to my feet. I wiped my eyes with the back of my hand to try and get the cum away, and he grabbed me by the neck.

"Bitch you thought I forgot you fought my son's mom and hurt my fucking son?" He said with his face close to mine. I started to cry.

"Nike, I swear I didn't mean to hurt your son. He ran up on me hitting me, and it was out of reflex. I would never hurt your son." I cried praying he believed me.

He let me go and smiled. "You know Evelynn I don't know why it was so hard for you to stay in your lane. I told you over and over to play your position."

He walked over to his desk and reached down and my eyes bucked. He pulled a gun out and sat on the edge of his desk with the gun in his lap.

"Nike, I'm sorry I just wanted you to see that I loved you. I would never have acted like that if you would have just been with me." I snapped.

"Eve, come on baby girl you're a hoe, what the fuck I look like wifing you? Half the niggas around here have had you and passed you." He said laughing.

"Fuck you, Nike! If your precious baby momma wouldn't have come back, you wouldn't be thinking that. I wonder how you would feel if she was gone for good."

I swear this nigga flew to me. He grabbed my neck again and pointed his gun at me. "Bitch did you just threaten my son's mom." I was scared shitless. I didn't say anything to afraid he might pull the trigger.

"Nah bitch don't get quiet now. Talk the shit you was just talking."

"I didn't mean anything by it. I just want you to see I'm the one for you!"

"Listen, you're lucky we're at my place of business because I would fucking shoot your hoe ass right here. So, I advise you to go back to wherever you been hiding and hide good because the next time I see you, I'm killing you, no conversations." He shoved me forward, and I stumbled.

"By the way, you got something on your face, he smirked, now get the fuck out." I turned and hurried to the door totally humiliated. I had cum all on my face and on top of that Shawn was right. Soon as I got in my car and drove off, I dialed his number and told him to meet me at my hideout.

I went there to try and warn Nike, and he played me so now I was going along with Shawn's plan. If he wanted to kill Nike who was I to stop him. He didn't give a fuck about me, and he just threatened my life, so I had to make sure Shawn got him before he got me.

CHAPTER 24

Noni

I had just got to the hospital to see about Trina. My mom agreed to keep KJ, and I was more than grateful. I looked and made sure my makeup was still covering the black eye Deshawn gave me and I made sure the scarf was covering the bruise on my neck. The swelling around my neck had gone down for the most part, and I was thankful.

I got to Trina's room and she was laying her bed sleep, and Momma T was sitting by her bed watching TV. I walked over and kissed her and took a seat next to her. "What are they saying?" I asked.

"They said her blood pressure was too high and she's at risk of being high risk." Momma T said.

I looked over at Trina and felt so bad for her. She wouldn't be going through this is she would just be honest with King and her and Duke could make up. I haven't seen her in about a week since she lied at Sunday dinner. I hadn't been around anyone because I didn't want them to see the marks on me.

I knew I had to tell King soon, Deshawn had been leaving lilies on my car and front door. I don't even know how he knows where I live. I was still kind of mad that Nike brought that bitch Taliyah to Sunday dinner when he knew his son and I were going to be there. So, I hadn't been talking to him. If I would have done that he would have tried to shoot me and dude.

I dropped KJ off to his moms and vice versa. I wasn't ready to face him and until I was, his moms was going to be our common ground.

I looked at Momma T, and she was staring at me funny. "Why are you looking at me like that?"

"Is everything okay?"

I laughed nervously and nodded my head. "Yeah of course." She side eyed me but didn't say anything. I tugged at my scarf and looked Trina.

"Where is Duke?" I asked.

"He's on his way home; his plane should be landing now."

I scrunched my face up. "Plane? Where he was at." She took a deep breath and told me the events that led up to us being here."

"Damn, they both need to get it together." I said shaking my head.

"They aren't the only ones. I don't know why you and Kingston are playing with each other. Y'all been doing this since y'all was in high school."

"No offense Momma T but your son is an asshole." I said rolling my eyes and crossing my legs.

"Yeah and you're childish, so I guess y'all both have things to work on." She said shrugging her shoulders.

"I am not childish," I yelled.

"First, calm your tone. Second, your little ass been running from my son since you been back. Now you got an attitude because he been with that little hussy. Which he's only flaunting her around to make you mad."

"Please, I don't care about him or her."

"You got to stop lying sis." Trina whispered and laughed. I hopped up and ran over to her.

"How you feeling sis?" I asked rubbing her stomach.

"Hungry, mom can you tell Nike to bring me some food when he comes up here."

"King's coming up here?" I asked.

"Duh, he's my brother, of course, he's coming." I crossed my arms across my chest but didn't respond, when someone busted through the door.

"Trina baby are you okay?" Duke said sounding out of breath.

She looked at him and rolled her eyes. "Why are you here Duke?"

"I came to make sure you and my baby were okay. What the fuck you mean?"

"Oh, you stopped fucking Farrah to come see me? After I've been calling you all fucking weekend!" She yelled.

"Trina watch you damn mouth and calm down before you shoot your blood pressure back up. Momma T said. You have no right to be mad at that boy after how you did him!"

"I do have a right, I'm pregnant with his baby, and he's been ignoring me four days! What if something was wrong and then he calls me just to let me hear him fucking another bitch! Fuck him."

"If yo ass wasn't in the hospital and at risk of losing my grandchild then I would beat your ass. Watch your fucking mouth." Momma T told her again and caused Trina to suck her teeth.

"I want Duke to leave; I don't need him to raise this baby with me. I got this."

He chuckled and grabbed the chair I was sitting in and moved it to the opposite side of the bed and sat it right next to her.

He leaned over and kissed her lips, and she jerked her head away causing him to laugh again.

"Y'all gone have my blood pressure high in a moment. They want to keep her overnight. Duke are you staying with her?" Momma T asked.

"No, he's leaving Noni can stay with me."

"I have to go get your nephew sis." I said quickly. I was lying, but she needed to talk to Duke."

"Well, mom you can stay." She said.

"Like hell I can, you have the father of your kid right next to you, and he's more than capable of staying with you."

She didn't wait for Trina to reply she just turned and headed towards the door but stopped and turned around.

"Duke, you better not stress my baby out anymore. Trina, I texted Nike and told him not to come up here. But you better tell him soon, it's not fair to Duke or your child, she turned and looked at me.

You better tell my son about your neck or tie your scarf better. I love you all, and I'll see y'all tomorrow."

She walked out the room, and Trina and Duke were staring at me when I turned and faced them.

"What's wrong with your neck?" Trina asked me.

I shook my head. "Girl nothing, I don't know what Momma T is talking about."

"Then take your scarf off." She said.

"Girl, I'm not about to entertain y'all. I got to go get my son. I'll be by to see you in the morning."

Duke was staring at me, then went to typing on his phone. I hoped he wasn't texting Nike because I didn't have the energy to deal with him right now.

I walked over and kissed Trina's cheek, and she almost choked my ass yanking on my scarf.

"Who the fuck choked you?" I pulled away from her and felt a scowl form on my lips.

"No one damn, bitch," I said.

"Aye, sis foreal. What the fuck happened to your neck?" Duke said staring at me.

"Nothing, y'all chill. I'm fine. I have to go." I didn't wait for either of them to respond, I just turned and walked out the room.

&

I sighed when I pulled into my house and seen Nike's car sitting outside. I got out my car and went straight for my door. I figured he had used his key and was in the house waiting on me. I walked in my house and didn't see him right away, but I heard him. I walked deeper into the house and realized he was upstairs.

I headed towards where I heard him moving around and opened

my bedroom door, and this nigga had the nerve to be sitting on my bed in a towel drinking a beer watching TV.

"King, what the fuck are you doing? And where the fuck are your clothes!" I yelled.

"My clothes got dirty earlier, and I was closer to your house, so I came here, they're in the washer." He didn't even look at me; his eyes never left the TV. I stared at his chocolate, tattooed covered stomach practically drooling. I eyed his perfectly toned arms remembering when he used to wrap them around me, that's the only time I truly ever felt safe. I walked deeper into my room and looked at the towel he was wearing, and his third leg sat perfectly on his thigh.

I looked up, and he was staring at me with a smirk. I quickly diverted my eyes from his and ran into the bathroom and slammed it shut. I pressed my back against the wall and clenched my legs together. It was a good thing I had jeans on because I would have had a puddle running down my leg.

I stripped out of my clothes and turned the shower on and hoped by the time I was finished King had put on some clothes.

I got in the shower and threw my head back as the water poured down on me I stuck my head under and enjoy the water beating on my scalp. I let my hands roam down my body and ran my fingers over my lower lips before slipping a finger inside.

My mind went back to King being laid out in my bed and how he used to stroke my pussy so good I was cumming in minutes. I began maneuvering my finger in and out of me and ran my other hand over my breast. I was so into what I was doing that I didn't notice or hear King come in.

"I knew I still got yo little hot ass horny. He said pressing his chest against my back and kissing my neck.

"King what are you doing." I moaned still playing with my pussy.

"What does it look like baby mama, I'm about to get reacquainted with my pussy." He started kissing down my back and grabbed my neck and bent me forward and dropped down. My body shook as soon as I felt his thick tongue graze across my pussy.

"Damn I missed this." He said into my pussy and pulled it into his mouth.

"Keep playing with that pussy baby." I did as I was told. King was eating my pussy from the back like he hadn't eaten in days. I felt myself about to cum and let it go when this nigga stuck his thumb in my ass and pulled my whole pussy in his mouth.

"King Fuck!" I yelled pulling my hand away from the between my legs and grabbing the wall.

He stood up and pulled me up and circled his hand around my waist and began playing with my clit. "King, please put it in baby," I begged. It's like every ounce of sense left once this man got close to me.

He pushed his dick in me, and I jumped forward. It had been a minute since I had sex and Nike was way bigger thank Shawn, so I knew this was about to hurt.

"Fuck Noni, you're so fucking tight." He groaned.

I felt him pull out some, then worked his way back in; he did this a couple of times until my body finally let him in, and I swear I was ready to marry his ass. He was hitting me with such long, strong strokes and I was cumming that fast.

He had one arm wrapped around me and brought the other one around my neck and pulled my head closer to him and leaned down.

"I can't believe you were giving this wet ass pussy to a fuck nigga."

"I'm sorry baby; I'm so sorry." He was sexing me so good my ass started crying.

"You're sorry huh? Daddy should punish you for giving his pussy away huh? He bit my ear and sped up.

"You gone go fuck another nigga again?" He asked still biting on my ear.

"No baby, I swear." I looped my arms back and wrapped them around his neck and turned to face him and kissed him.

He shoved his tongue into my mouth, and I welcomed it and sucked on it. "I'm about to cum again baby!" I moaned in his mouth.

"Me too cum with me Noni." I looked up and looked in eyes, and he started playing with my breast and pinched my nipples, and I came hard as hell starring in his eye, and he came right after me. My body shook, and I felt my knees buckle, and King grabbed me.

I turned around and wrapped my arms around his neck and kissed him. "I love you," I said into his mouth.

He pulled back and put his forehead on mine, "I love you too." He pecked my lips again and pulled away, he looked at me, and his eyes got dark and a frown formed on his face.

"Where the fuck did those bruises come from?" Damn, I forgot all about those. I knew he was about to flip shit when I told him.

CHAPTER 25

*N*ike

I grabbed Noni's chin and turned her face up and looked at it and then at her neck. I felt myself about to lose it. "Who the fuck put their hands on you?"

Her left eye was black, and when I lifted her neck you could see it was bruised too! "Let's get out the shower, and I'll tell you. I can't focus while you're naked." She said snatching from me.

I grabbed the rag I used earlier, and my body wash I had brought and began washing up. If I wasn't so pissed, I would have slid back up in Noni, watching the suds run down her body made me want to fuck her ass senseless, but that would have to wait.

Once we were both showered and dressed, I sat on Noni's bed and watched her watch me. I was trying my hardest to keep my anger at bay because I remember the last time I got mad and scared her.

"Start talking Shonni," I said.

"Deshawn's here in Miami" She whispered avoiding eye contact.

"Come again?" I said.

"Deshawn, he was sending me threatening text messages, and then a few days ago he popped up at my school."

"Why the fuck didn't you tell me?"

"I was going to I swear. I just was so mad about you bringing ol girl to dinner that I wasn't ready to face you. But then I started getting lilies on my porch and car, and I knew I had to tell you."

"I'm confused what does that have to do with anything?" I asked.

She rolled her eyes. "Lillie's are my favorite flower Nike, and Deshawn knows that. The day he came to my school he brought me some, but once he started threatening you and telling me how he wasn't leaving without me, I slapped them out his hand and laughed in his face. That's when he." She stopped and looked down at her hands.

"That's when he what?" I said rising off the bed and walked over to her.

"He punched me like I was some random nigga on the street and then grabbed me by my neck." She started crying, and I pulled her into me and stroked her back.

I was trying to get Shonni to calm down when it clicked in my head. "You said you're getting Lillie's on your porch and shit, right?" I said pulling her back and looking at her." She slowly nodded her head.

I let her go and began pacing. "Shonni that means that nigga knows where the fuck you live. Where the fuck my son lives! You should have been come to me!" I yelled facing her.

"I know I fucked up. I'm sorry, I was just so mad, but I swear I was gonna tell you!"

"You're so fucking selfish! This is the fucking second time you put my son in danger when it came to this nigga because you were in your feelings. How long was he sending you the text messages?"

"For about a month." She said lowly.

"A fucking month Shonni!"

"I fucked up I know, I'm sorry. I didn't think he would actually find me. It's been almost a year since I last seen him, so when he started texting me again, I blew it off. How was I supposed to know he would really find me?"

"Shonni for you to be so fucking book smart, you lack common sense. That nigga wasn't just sending threats out of nowhere for his fucking health. Look you and KJ are going back to my house, and I don't want to hear no shit from you about it."

Surprisingly she didn't give me a fuss about it. She nodded her head and headed to her closet and grabbed a bag and I turned to her dresser where my phone was going off. I walked over to it and looked to see who it was. It was Taliyah, I was supposed to go over her house, but she had to get put on the back burner, my family needed me, and nobody came before Shonni and my son.

Plus, she was annoying as hell. She always wanted to be up my ass, and I was sick of it. Fucking her wasn't even all that, she better be lucky she could suck a mean dick or she was gonna get the boot. It didn't matter though because soon as I took care of this nigga Deshawn, I was getting my family back. That nigga better enjoys his life right now because I was determined to find him and make him regret ever putting hands on my girl.

&.

*J*called Duke and asked him to meet at my house the next morning, and he agreed and said soon as he left the hospital. I wondered why he was at the hospital, speaking of hospitals I needed to check on my sister.

I dialed her number, and she answered whispering to someone in the background.

"Hey Nike." She said, finally paying attention to the phone.

"What's up big head girl?"

"Please, you got yo nerve talking about someone's head."

I laughed, it was nice hearing her sound like she was doing okay.

"How you feeling?" I asked.

"I'm fine, they want to keep me one more night because my pressure is still kind of high, but my baby is fine."

I heard someone say something in the background.

"Aye, was that Duke?" I asked.

"Uh, yeah he stopped by here to see me."

"How did he know you were in the hospital?"

135

"I uh, I called him and asked him to bring me something to eat." I guess made sense Duke was just as much as Trina brother as I was.

"Well tell that nigga I said hurry up, it's important."

She yelled to get his attention and told him what I said. "So, did you see Noni's neck?"

"Man, hell yeah, how did you know?"

"Mommy noticed it when she came up to the hospital, and I pulled on her scarf after mom made a comment about."

"I'm mad as fuck that nigga got that close to her!"

"Who got that close?"

"She didn't tell you who did it? It was her punk ass ex. That nigga is here in Miami."

"What! I hope you're looking for him."

"Come on sis you know me better than that. Matter fact I'm about to go check on her. I'll be up to see you later on."

"Okay, bye love you."

"Love you too." I hung up and tossed my phone on the couch and headed upstairs to check on Noni.

I walked in my bedroom, and she was sprawled out with her ass tooted in the air. Her hair was spread all over her face, and she only had on a pair of panties and a sports bra. I knew her ass was gone sleep in late, she was up crying half the night and refused to let me leave her side once she finally calmed down. I was still pissed she didn't tell me that nigga was in town but I put that to the side because she was already beating herself up.

The longer I stared at her, the harder my dick got. Before yesterday it had been four years since I had been in Noni and I swear her shit was molded for me. My dick fit her like a glove, and she was always wet and tight as fuck. I was hoping last night I got her ass pregnant again, I purposely didn't pull out. If she didn't get pregnant last night, then I'm going to have to keep letting off inside her until she becomes pregnant. The longer I stared at her, the more I had the desire to be in her.

I pulled my shorts and boxers I was wearing down and began stroking my dick. I walked up to my bed and climbed on it. I got behind Noni and slide her panties to the side and began rubbing her clit with my thumb. She fidgeted and a moan escaped her mouth, but she didn't open her eyes. I bent down and kissed her pussy lips and ran my tongue over it.

"King." She moaned out.

I pulled up and bit my lip and grabbed her hips with one hand and held my dick in the other. I placed myself at her opening and ran my dick up and down her slit enjoying seeing her juices coat the tip of my dick. She still had her eyes closed, but she started moving herself backward. I knew she wanted me to enter her.

"You want this dick baby momma?" I asked slapping her ass.

"Yes please." She whined.

"How bad you want it."

"Nike, come on stop playing!"

I laughed because I hated when she called me Nike. I finally quit teasing her and put this dick in her life.

I grabbed her hips with each hand and began rolling my hips into her. She was matching my stroke, and she arched her back more, and I had to think of something else before I busted.

Watching her ass jiggle as I slammed into her was a beautiful sight. I pulled half my dick and out and seen her juices coating it. I reached around and began playing with her clit.

"Damn Noni quit squeezing my dick like that."

"King, don't stop please!" Her pussy got tighter on my dick, and I knew she was about to cum. I pulled out, and she looked at me with the deadliest stare.

I chuckled. "Chill I want you on top." I laid next to where she was laying and pulled her up and on me. She slowly slid down on my pole and stood on her feet and placed her hands on my chest and started bouncing up and down. I grabbed her waist trying to slow her down because I wasn't trying to cum yet.

"Shit, Noni slow down." But her ass threw her head back and rocked her hips as if she had an imaginary beat in her head.

"King I'm about to cum. Can I cum baby?" She looked down at me. I bit my lip and nodded. I gripped her waist and started humping her from below. Her body began to shake, and her pussy tightened around my dick, and I shot my seeds in her. I made sure I held her in place, so all my soldiers hit a target.

She clasped on top of me and kissed me. "Hey." She said with a goofy grin on her face.

"You're such a cornball get off me," I said laughing.

I pecked her lips, and she rolled over and stretched.

"I can get used to waking up to this." She grabbed my dick and squeezed it.

I laughed again. "Come on little horny ass girl, let's continue this in the shower."

I got up and walked over to where she was and picked her up and headed to my bathroom.

After two more rounds in the shower Noni and I got dressed and headed downstairs and Duke was sitting on the couch on his phone.

"Damn nigga I forgot yo ass was coming over," I said laughing.

"Yo ass was too busy blowing sis's back out." He said with a grin and looked at her.

"Duke shut up!" Her cheeks turned red, and she hurried into the kitchen. Duke looked in the direction she headed then back at me and handed me my phone.

"That Taliyah bitch been blowing you up and Evelyn called. The fuck you doing talking to her." He whispered while checking for Noni. I titled my head telling him to follow me. I walked past the kitchen and down the hall to my office I had in the back of the house. I explained to him how Evelynn came to see me and how I had someone following her since she left my shop.

"The dumb bitch wants to be with me so bad that she thought I would really forgive her after it was her fault my son had to staples in his head," I said.

"Yeah that bitch dumb as fuck, so when you going to handle her."

"Soon as I deal with Shonni's ex, I'm going after that bitch. Speaking of him, he found Shonni and put his fucking hands on her." Every time I thought about the marks on Noni I wanted to snap that niggas neck. They were fading, but you can still see them. It made sense why her ass stayed away from me, she tried to make it seem like it was because of Taliyah, which I admit it was childish of me to bring her dinner, but I needed Noni to see I wasn't waiting forever.

"How we gone handle dude?" Duke asked snapping me out of thoughts.

"First we got to find out what he looks like then you know money talks. I'm putting a price on his head. It seems like that fuck nigga is obsessed with Noni, so he's not going to stay away from her."

He nodded his head and his phone rang. "Aye, I got to head out but, let me know when you want to handle both situations and you know I'm down." He stood up, and we pounded fist.

I followed him out the door and down the hall back to the front of the house. He said his goodbyes to Noni and headed out the door.

CHAPTER 26

*D*uke

I stopped by Trina's house to grab her an overnight bag so she could have something to wear later on. I grabbed her hygiene stuff and noticed she had a man body wash in her bathroom. I picked it up and examined it. It damn sure wasn't mine, so it better have belonged to her brother, or I was going to fuck someone up.

I tossed the body wash in the bag too. She was about to explain what nigga she had in her house and she better hoped I accepted the answer.

I grabbed the rest of the things I needed from her house and lifted my vibrating phone out my pocket, and it was Farrah. This was the first time she tried to contact me since I left her house. I debated if I was going to answer and bit the bullet and picked up.

"What Farrah?" I asked soon as I answered. I walked to the front of Trina's house and walked out the door making sure I locked the door.

"Hey Duke, are you busy." She said quietly.

"I actually am."

"Okay, I just wanted to apologize for how I acted yesterday. I was completely out of line." I didn't say anything though. I walked to my car and put Trina's bag in the passenger seat started my car.

"Duke are you there?" She asked.

"Yeah, look Farrah the shit you pulled wasn't cool, I could have lost my fucking child because you wanted to be childish as fuck. I can't fuck with that."

"I know Duke, and I'm sorry. Is the baby okay?"

"Look, I got to go. Don't call me anymore, I'm trying to make it work with my baby mom."

"You're kidding, right? You just spent the whole weekend with me, and now you think you're about to kick me to the curb."

I ran my hand over my face. "I'm trying to be as nice as possible because I respect you Farrah, but your pushing it. Don't fucking call my phone again." I hung up and backed out Trina's driveway and headed back to the hospital.

"What took you so long." Were Trina's first words when I walked in her room.

"I had a few stops to make before I came back up here," I said and handed her, her bag.

I sat down in the chair by her bed and watched her as she began pulling the contents out her bag. When she got to the guy's body was she scrunched her face up and looked at me.

"Why did you bring your body wash and no clothes?" She asked.

I raised my eye brow at her. She had me fucked up, and she didn't even know it.

"That's not my body wash," I said with an even voice.

"Well, who's is it?" She asked.

"You tell me. What nigga been staying at your house that he felt the need to leave his fucking body wash!" I yelled jumping up.

She jumped and looked back at the body wash. Her eyes widen, and she looked at me.

"What nigga you been fucking while you're pregnant with my baby Trina?" Before she could answer, there was a knock on the door and the same nigga she was at the mall with came in.

I cut my eyes at her. She had me so fucked up right now. She just spazzed out on me for being with Farrah, and she was still fucking with ol boy.

141

"Why the fuck are you here?" I asked stepping towards him.

"Duke please not here. Trina said. Ashur, I told you I was fine."

"Why are you still even talking to him?"

"The same reason why you were fucking that bitch!"

I pinched the bridge of my nose and tried to calm myself down.

"Yo, you got to get the fuck out and don't come back around my baby mom."

"Trina didn't ask me to leave, and I want to make sure she was okay." He said walking on the opposite side of the bed from where I was and grabbed her hand.

I laughed and shook my hand. Her eyes widen again, and she looked from me to her hand and snatched it out of his.

"Look, I'm trying to keep calm because I don't need her stressed out again, but you got three seconds to walk yo ass out back out the fucking door, or I'm going to react."

He must have took me as a joke because he crossed his arms across his chest. I quickly reached behind me and grabbed my gun. I had gotten it out the glove compartment of my car earlier before coming back to visit Trina, and pointed it at him."

"Now like I said get the fuck out. I'll shoot yo ass, and then pay the hospital to cover it up play with me." I cocked my gun and smiled.

"Duke, what the fuck! Put that away before someone walks in." Trina yelled. I ignored her. Seeing him that close to her had me wanting to black out and I wasn't trying to go there.

He looked like he was about to shit his pants. He stood there and was a still as a statue. "Ashur please leave! What the fucking are you still standing there for!" Trina yelled at him. She got out her bed and stood in front of me.

"Duke, baby please put the gun away." I didn't take my eyes off ol boy though. "Get the fuck out!" Trina yelled at him, and he jumped and hurried out the room. She grabbed my wrist, and I made eye contact with her put my gun back on safety and put it down slowly. She wrapped her arms around my waist and dug her face in my chest.

"Please don't ever scare me like that again." I felt a wet spot on my shirt, and I looked down at her. I heard her sniffling. I hugged her, with the gun still in my hand.

"I'm sorry," I said. She looked up at me.

"The body wash was Ashur's he stayed the night with me a few times, but I haven't slept with him since I found out I was pregnant." I lowered my face down to hers.

"I see him around you again, and I'm killing him no questions asked. I said. You've seen me black out, and I don't like going to that place, but I promise you, you're the one who will make that happen." I didn't wait for her to answer I dipped down and kissed her.

I slipped my tongue into her mouth and sucked on her bottom lip. I moved in closer, and I felt something hit me. I jumped back and looked down.

"What the fuck was that? I yelled.

"Oh, my gosh Duke that was the baby it kicked." She squealed.

She grabbed my hand and placed it on her stomach, and there was a little thump.

I felt tears forming in my eyes. I don't give a fuck what anyone said feeling you child grow like this was amazing.

"Damn, I love you." I blurted out. She looked up at me with her mouth wide open.

"Do you mean that?" She said.

"Come on Trina when did you ever know me to say shit I didn't mean." She moved back and placed her hands over her mouth and started crying again.

"Aye, what the fuck is wrong with you."

"I love you too; I was just scared to tell you." I smiled and walked closer to her and snatched her up in my arms and crushed my lips against hers.

"I'm sorry about what you heard," I said against her mouth.

"Are you still going to be fucking her?" She asked.

"Nah, I cut that off. I want this Trina; I don't want to see you with anyone else. I want to raise our kid together, and I don't want you talking to the nigga."

She nodded her head. "I want this too Duke, but I'm scared. I don't want you to feel like you have to be with me because we're having a baby."

"I admit that crossed my mind, but I knew the first time I slid in you foreal. You're beautiful as fuck, and I've always thought that. You speak your mind, and you love hard. Shit, and got some bomb ass pussy too." She laughed and hit my arm.

"But foreal, I want this, but you have to tell your brother about us," I said pulling away from her.

"I know, and I'm going to." I stared at her hoping she was telling the truth. I wanted to see if this would go somewhere but I couldn't keep sneaking behind my nigga's back.

*

We were currently waiting for Trina's lab work to come back. I was tired of sleeping in this hospital. I looked over at her, and she was peacefully sleeping. Last night she promised that she was going to tell Nike about us and I hoped she knew that meant soon.

I was currently looking through my phone. We had a meeting tonight, and I was making sure everyone was aware. We had a big project score coming up, and we couldn't afford any mess ups.

"Who got yo ass so focused over there." I looked up, and Trina was staring at me.

I got up and walked over to her and rubbed my hand over her stomach.

"Yo ass better get over that jealousy shit." I smiled at her and kissed her, and the door busted in. I swear I couldn't wait to go home no one respected privacy in this mutha fucka.

"Yo what the fuck is going on." I felt Trina tense up and I pulled away from her and looked over and into the stare of Nike.

"Listen bro-." I started.

"It's not what it looks like!" Trina said quickly.

I whipped my head in her direction. Noni walked in and looked from Nike to us.

"What's going on?" She asked.

"I just fucking walked in on Duke kissing my fucking sister."

She didn't say anything back, and he looked at her.

"You know what's going on don't you?" He asked her, but she still didn't answer.

"Trina, it's now, or I'm out." I threatened. She looked from between me and Nike.

"Nike is the father of my baby." She said more to herself.

He stepped closer and glared at me. "Say that one more time. I think you just said Duke, my best friend, fuck that my brother, your brother is the father of my niece or nephew."

"Listen, bro let me explain." That was all I got out before he rocked me in my jaw.

"My fucking sister! You fucked my sister!" I knew he was pissed, but he had me fucked up. I recovered quickly and sent a two piece his way.

"STOP!" Trina and Noni yelled, but both of us were too hype. We were matching each other blow for blow. Someone must have seen us through the open door or called about the noise because security came in and grabbed me us apart from one another.

"Nigga, out of all the bitches you fucked my sister and got her pregnant!" Nike yelled.

"You act like I fucked yo bitch, Trina's grown as fuck."

"We're going to have to escort both of you off the premises." One of the guards. Trina hopped off the bed and ran over to Nike.

"Nike, please don't be mad, I love Duke, and I'm sorry this happen, but there's nothing we could do about it now." She walked over to me, and I snatched away from the guard holding me, and she wrapped her arms around me.

"Are you okay?" She asked looking up at me.

I nodded and kissed her forehead. Nike didn't say anything, he snatched away from the guard and pushed him away and stalked out the room.

"I'll talk to him. Call me when you get home Trina." Noni said and rushed after Nike.

"Y'all might as well leave because until my girl is discharged, I'll be right here." They looked at each other and shrugged and walked out.

Trina touched my left cheek, and I flinched. Nike had got me got me good with that first punch. I leaned down and kissed her.

"I love you," I said.

She wiped her eyes and smiled. "I love you too."

I would just let Nike calm down, this was the first time we had ever come to blows, and I hoped he could accept this and it would be soon.

CHAPTER 27

*N*oni

"King hold up damn!" I yelled after him. His tall ass was walking fast as fuck, and I was struggling to keep up with him. We were outside and was walking through the parking lot to his car.

He stopped and turned to face me. "You knew, didn't you?" He asked.

"Yeah, but Trina wanted to tell you."

"Fuck that; you should have told me! Why is it that your always fucking hiding something from me!"

"King, that wasn't for me to tell you. Trina wanted to tell you."

"The day at dinner you knew she was lying, didn't you?"

I didn't respond, but instead, I nodded my head.

"I swear, you are the most untrustworthy bitch I have ever fucked with!" My heart quickened.

"King, I didn't even do anything! I get your mad, but you're not about to talk to me like your fucking crazy."

He looked at me and crossed his arms. "You're just as guilty as them two mutha fucka. All three of yall can stay the fuck away from me." He turned and started walking towards his car again.

"Wait where are you going?" I yelled.

"You're not my bitch so don't worry about it." He got to his car and started it and sped off. I sat there mouth wide open, and tears threatening to fall.

I turned and walked back into the hospital and headed back to Trina's room. I walked in, and Duke was in the bed, and Trina was lying next to him.

"I thought yall left. Nike isn't bringing his hostile ass back in here is he?" Trina said sitting up.

I shook my head and walked over to one of the chairs and sat down, and started crying in my hands.

"What's wrong?" She got out the bed and was now rubbing my back. I looked up from my hands and up at her and smiled when I focused in on her belly.

"Yeah Noni, what's up?" Duke asked.

"King left me here," I said.

"What you mean he left you?" Duke asked.

I told them what was said and started to cry all over again.

"Noni I'm sorry," Trina said.

I shook my head. "It's not your fault. He's still mad about Deshawn, and this just gave him a reason to express it." I blew a breath out.

"Do you mind dropping me off at his house?" I asked Duke.

"You know I got you, sis."

Two hours later they had finally released Trina and Duke had dropped me off at King's house. I didn't see his car and was grateful. I didn't feel like arguing with him. If I weren't so scared Deshawn would find me, I would go home, but that would only make things worse.

I walked in the house and called my mom to see if she wanted me to come get KJ but she told me he was fine. I was glad because I didn't want to argue in front of him when King got back. He had seen enough of Deshawn and I, so I wasn't trying to do it with his dad too.

I walked upstairs and sat on King's bed when I walked in his room and pulled my phone out. I went to his contact and dialed his number, but it went straight to voicemail. I tried two more times before I gave up. I stripped out my clothes and got in the shower and hoped King would be home by the time I got out.

It was one in the morning, and King's ass still wasn't home or answering. I was getting pissed off and wanted to beat his ass. I was laying down when I got a notification that my silent alarm was set off I went to the app and put my code in before the people were notified.

I tried to call Nike one last time, and he didn't answer again, so I sent him a 911 text at my house and told him to meet me there. I jumped up and headed to the closet and put on one of my Nike sweat suits and my all black Huaraches. I grabbed my phone and keys and headed down to my car and to my house.

I pulled up in my driveway and didn't see anything out the ordinary. I got out and walked up to the door, and someone pulled up. I turned around, and King was getting out his car. I mugged him and rolled my eyes.

"What's going on? He asked walking up.

"Where the fuck have you been?" I asked.

"Look, I didn't come here for this, what's going on?"

"I don't know, I got an alert my alarm went off, and here we are."

"So, you were just going to going to come investigate by yourself?"

"You weren't answering your phone!" I yelled.

He didn't respond. He snatched my keys away from me and pushed me out the way and unlocked the door. He pulled a gun from the back of his pants, walked in, and I followed.

"Wait here." He said and went deeper in the house.

A few minutes later he called out to me, and I walked in the direction he called me.

"Someone was definitely in here; your back door was wide open." He said. I looked around, and nothing was out of place.

"Do you think they're still here?" I whispered.

"I don't know, but I'm going to find out." He closed the door and turned to me.

"Don't leave the kitchen." He walked back to the front of the house and heard some doors open, the bathroom, closet, and bedroom that was downstairs, I heard him head upstairs, and I headed to the front of the house.

A couple of minutes passed and I heard his talking to someone. I couldn't hear too much, but I knew it was a male. I walked closer to the stairs and heard Deshawn's voice. I grabbed my phone and dialed Duke's number.

"Duke who the fuck is calling you at almost two in the morning," Trina yelled in the background.

"Shut the fuck up Trina; it's Noni. He said. What's up sis?"

"Duke I need you to get to my house!" I broke down to him what was going on.

"I don't know what to do."

"Pull the trigger bitch." I heard King yell and I couldn't stay put anymore.

"Duke hurry!" I dropped my phone and took off up the stairs.

CHAPTER 28

*D*eshawn

I had been sitting outside Shonni's house for the past two nights, and the bitch had yet to show up. I was beyond pissed; the bitch wonders why I have to beat her ass and shit like this.

I parked a couples of houses down from her crib, I grabbed my book bag and walked towards her house. It was close to one in the morning, so there wasn't a lot going on. I walked up her driveway and to the back of her house. I walked up to her back door and pulled my book bag from off my back and grabbed my lock picking kit.

Once, I got the door opened I walked in and started to check inside her drawers in the kitchen. I was trying to find some kind of indication where that nigga Kingston lived; I knew that was where she was. I looked in all the rooms downstairs and found nothing. I walked in the living room and instantly got pissed. This bitch had pictures of her, KJ, and Kingston all around in her house like they were some big ass family.

I walked to the stairs and headed up there and looking for Shonni's room. I knew there had to be something with this nigga's address in here. I finally had found her room and was looking through her nightstand, Shonni always kept her important papers in her night stand when we lived together. I was going through the papers when I heard the front door open. I froze and listened to what sounded like Noni, and I'm guessing her punk ass baby dad. I heard them moving around downstairs and knew I had to hurry up.

I threw the paper on the bed not seeing anything helpful and walked over to her dresser and started looking through it. I heard steps getting closer to the stairs and ran to the closet and hid inside. I looked over and seen a bat and picked it up. Kingston had walked into the room and walked right to the bed looking at the papers. He walked in the bathroom, and I opened the door slowly and stood on the side of the bathroom door.

Soon as I seen him coming out, I swung the bat and hit in the stomach causing him to hunch over and grab his stomach and dropped his gun. I threw the bat across the room and hurried and picked up the gun and pointed it at him.

He looked up and tried to get his breathing under control.

"Andre, what the fuck are you doing?" He said slowly, still catching his breath.

I laughed. "Nigga I'm the nigga you been looking for," I said.

He looked and then a scowl grazed his lips.

"Your Noni's ex?"

"Yep, your dumbass had me in your shop and ain't even know." He launched at me, and I cocked the gun.

"Take one more step, and I'll kill you. I mean I plan on killing you anyways so now would be perfect."

"Nigga, I swear if you shoot me you better kill me. I already owe you a bullet for my son and Noni."

"Nigga, fuck your bastard ass son. I should have made Shonni give his ass up for adoption."

"Put the gun away and fight me, my nigga. You loved beating Noni's ass, so beat mine."

"Noni didn't fucking listen, if she did I wouldn't have had to beat her. It's fine soon as I get you out the way I'm taking her back to Atlanta and teaching her ass a lesson she'll never forget.

"Well pull the trigger bitch." The minute he said that everything happened so fast. He ran towards me, and I pulled the trigger hitting him in the shoulder he stopped and grabbed it. I aimed the gun at his head this time.

"DESHAWN NO!" I smiled because Shonni was about to see her son's father die at my hands.

"KING MOVE!" Noni ran and jumped in front of him pushing him as I pulled the trigger.

POW.

I watched in horror as the bullet rip through Shonni's chest, and she dropped to the ground.

SHONNI!!!!!!!!

TO BE CONTINUED...

CPSIA information can be obtained
at www.ICGtesting.com
Printed in the USA
LVHW05s1134290418
575300LV00013B/825/P